HYLAND'S CONSORT

A RAGE AND REVENGE NOVEL

A DARK MAFIA DARK NECESSITIES ROMANCE
BOOK TWO

FELICITY BRANDON

Copyright © 2021 by Felicity Brandon
This is a work of fiction. Names, characters, places, and incidents either are the product of the author's imagination or are used fictitiously. Any resemblance to actual persons, living or dead, events, or locales is entirely coincidental.
All rights reserved. No part of this book may be reproduced or used in any manner without written permission of the copyright owner except for the use of quotations in a book review. For more information, address: felicitybrandon@felicitybrandonauthor.com
This book is entirely a work of fiction.
The author does not condone, nor endorse any of the acts in this book.
First edition October 2021

Cover design by Raven Designs.
Editing by Personal Touch Editing.
Formatting by Format the Forbidden

Download your FREE Felicity book here.
https://felicitybrandonauthor.com/

SEXY FREE READS

Sign up for my newsletter and receive FREE sexy reads
here!
https://felicitybrandonwrites.com/newsletter/

I loved him.
I hated him.
But could I live without him?

PROLOGUE: SEAN HYLAND

"You're sure this is what you want?" His expression serious, Crane's fingers paused over the keyboard as he glanced up.

"Are you asking if I'm mentally competent?" I sniggered, amused the man I paid such a huge sum was questioning me.

"I'm asking if you're sure." His fingers went to work again, *tap, tap, tapping* on the plastic keys as he completed the paperwork. "I'd be remiss if I didn't, sir. It's all so…" He paused, apparently trying to think of the right word.

"Sudden?" My brow arched. He was right. The decision to take a wife was abrupt, to say the least, and contrary to the self-serving man I'd become, but Hilary had turned everything upside down. Since I got my hands on her, all I could think about was leading her down the aisle and finally claiming what was mine.

"Precisely." Crane leaned forward, staring at me over his spectacles. "I've known you a long time, Mr. Hyland." His tone was ominous, reminding me of one of my uncle Zander's droning speeches… until Saul Morrison had put a bullet through Zander's brain. "And I knew your uncle even longer. I just want to ensure your interests are protected."

"That's exactly what you're going to do," I assured him, offering the older man a smile. "You'll ensure all Zander's properties and assets are safeguarded in the event of divorce or my death."

"They're your assets now, sir."

"That's right." I sighed, leaning back in the huge black leather seat. I still hadn't wrapped my head around Zander's death, let alone avenged the bastard who'd brought him down, but I would. I was working on both, and my new bride was the pièce de résistance. "Sometimes, it's difficult to think about it that way."

Crane considered me from behind the vast screen. "That's understandable." His tone was sympathetic. "The loss of Mr. Hyland was tragic. None of us want to believe he's gone."

Yet he was gone—murdered in the same grotty London office I was redecorating, brought to heel by the rival gang who'd been the thorn in his side his whole life.

"Still, you're here now." Crane's lips twitched. "The next generation of Hyland, and I feel sure there're brighter days to come."

"Indeed, there are." I pressed my fingertips together, contemplating the day in question. The wedding was set in only three days, and the documents Crane was putting together were the final loose ends to be tied up. "A great many. I thank you for your concern, Mr. Crane, as well as your long service, but my mind is made up. I'm marrying Miss Mantle."

His brow rose at my emphatic tone, but a professional like Crane knew when to argue and when to get the job done. "Very good, sir." He pressed his lips together, attention flitting back to the screen. "Then we're nearly done here. I'll just need a signature from Miss Mantle."

"An electronic one won't suffice?" I already knew the answer, but I asked anyway. Getting Hilary to Crane's office was going to be an interesting challenge. I'd been keeping her in sensory deprivation, edging her closer and closer to ecstasy each time we played but never permitting her to reach the stars. After so long without the light, without hope and longing for my touch, Hilary had become quite the well-trained, eager pup. I could certainly get her to sign the paperwork, but taking her from the place I held her wasn't my preferred option.

"I'm afraid not," he replied. "I could bring the papers to your address if you desire?"

"No, I'll bring her here." I sighed, but even as the air was expelled, my lips curled, imagining my gorgeous blonde scampering around on all fours in Crane's wood-paneled office. "She could use a trip out."

Crane laughed. "Well, I've never heard my offices referred to that way, sir."

My grin widened at his amusement. "These are strange times, Mr. Crane. I'm certain Hilary will appreciate the chance to meet you."

"Very good," he replied, his focus flitting between the screen and my face. "Does tomorrow suit you both? Better we get this finalized in advance of the wedding, I think."

"Tomorrow is grand."

I envisioned Hilary's slender limbs moving across Crane's old-fashioned carpet and her utter embarrassment at the public humiliation, but she may as well get used to it. Come the big day, she'd be bared and subjugated as much as I desired, and based on the way I was constantly aroused, that could be most of the day.

"What time, Mr. Crane?"

"I have an early slot." He peered around the screen as if checking I was still there. Poor Derek Crane. I'd be willing to wager his office had never seen anything like my bride-to-be. "Nine in the morning?"

I inhaled at the thought of having to drag Hilary here so early. "I can make that work," I agreed, trying to ignore the swell of passion that surged at the thought of Hilary and focusing on the dry, monotonous, but nonetheless significant reasons that brought me to Crane's office. "It will give you the chance to meet my intended and see what all the fuss is about."

"Yes, sir, though I'm sure she's quite the catch. Why else would you want to get her down the aisle so quickly?" He grinned, revealing a line of crooked teeth, and I started to laugh.

"Why else, indeed?"

CHAPTER 1: HILARY MANTLE

The slither of illumination at the far end of the room edged across the wall. Cast from the tiny space behind the blackout blind, which leaked light, it was only a trickle, but it was all I had. In the days I'd been here, I noticed its pattern and envied it. I resented its routine, begrudged the fact it could move so freely when I could not, but over time, it had come to represent something greater than just the contrast between our fortunes—it began to indicate time. Based on its position, I could work out what time of day it was beyond the endless gloom of the place where he kept me, its presence a fleeting semblance of normality in this new depravity.

Sighing, I watched its slow path, tension knotting in my shoulders. I was naked and bound to the chair again. I was always bound and naked. Tethered and unable to flee, enveloped in sultry shadows and, as usual, right on the edge of reason before I'd been abandoned. Fleetingly, my mind flitted back to the first day Sean Hyland had captured me, to the onslaught I'd been made to endure at his hands, the rounds and rounds of pleasure he'd ripped from my reluctant body in that dank little basement cell. That might as well have been a thousand years ago for all I could recall of the thunderous orgasms. Now, those climaxes were as out of reach as freedom itself. It was the game Sean loved to play—one that enthralled him while leaving me perpetually on the brink of breakdown. Each time he returned, I'd be permitted to move, but liberty came at a price. I'd have to cede to his demented will and allow him access to my body, permit him to torment me. There was no denying Sean could play the game. He was a champion competitor. We'd only just met, yet he was capable of stimulating me in ways most men could hardly conceive, and while he'd refrained from actually taking what he so clearly believed belonged to him, the threat was always there. *I was his.* His to tease, his to harass, his to garner thrills from, and one day, he would expect much more.

My insides tightened at the thought of that day. Sean had made no bones about it. It would be our wedding day, and apparently, it was looming faster than I imagined, though in the confines of this place, even the slither of light couldn't illuminate how soon for me.

"Soon," I whispered into the darkness, pleased for once, he'd permitted me the possibility.

Sean had a penchant for gags and enjoyed seeing me struggle in one. It was all shades of wrong, watching him harden at my dismay at not being able to communicate, but even worse was the pulverizing reality I enjoyed it, too. What could be worse than finding yourself in such a hopeless situation—hostage to the deranged rival of your boss—than discovering you actually relished his insidious attention? But it was true. I'd been wetter and needier than ever fettered in his bondage. Hornier than I'd been with any boyfriend and even needier than I'd been with Saul. My face screwed up at the unpleasant reality. Saul Morrison, the man who'd signed my paychecks for the last three years, was also the same man I'd bedded by choice before this ordeal—the man I thought I'd been in love with.

Where was Saul?

Glancing up, my gaze fixed on the dribble of light visible across the room. Was he out there somewhere, looking for me? Granted, we never got to the stage of saying we loved each other, and I wasn't sure either of us was ready to declare undying devotion, but we'd been pretty damn close. If I knew anything about my lover, he protected everyone in his organization. He'd come for me—I knew he would—he'd never leave me to rot in the darkness with a ruthless cretin like Sean Hyland. That wasn't Saul's style. However, he wouldn't anticipate how deep the rabbit hole had gone, wouldn't dare guess at the devious games Sean played. Never in Saul's wildest dreams would he imagine the nephew of his old gang rival would not only capture me but plan to marry me.

Once I was Mrs. Hyland, where could I go from there? There could be no coming back, no divorce lawyer who could wash away the stain of having actually been his wife. How could I go back to Saul's organization, The Syndicate, after that? How could I go back to his bed? The short answer was, I couldn't. If Sean insisted on this lunacy, he was forcing my hand into more than just marriage. He was imposing an entirely new life on me, a new job, a new social circle—if he ever allowed me out of this bloody room.

A shot of anger raced through me, my impotency swelling until it was difficult to take another breath. I still couldn't believe this had happened. I'd been content with my life in a job I enjoyed with a decent group of friends. I'd finally found a man who respected me, a man I could envision a real future with, then this had happened. Now I was lucky if I could leave my damn chair, and when I did, Sean had me crouching over a bowl to relieve myself before I begged and pleaded for more of whatever pleased him.

If you'd have told me only a couple of weeks ago that this would be my fate, I'm certain I would have called you crazy, but not only was I Sean's prisoner, in the haze of shadows and craving for the satisfaction he never offered, I couldn't even contemplate how to escape. My head was a mess, spinning with every sound. Was that the creaking floorboard Sean approaching from behind the door? Was he about to arrive and turn my world on its head again?

Yes, he met my basic needs. He ensured I was fed and as clean as water and a sponge could achieve, but this neverending solitude was starting to drive me insane. Hours when only the noise of my frantic heartbeat kept me company, that and the slow progress of the slither of light— my only friend in this dark desolation. It had gotten to the point where I no longer knew what I wanted, wasn't sure if I longed for Sean's arrival, for human interaction, to be free of the chair at least. Or if I craved the boundless hours of seclusion, the time when I only had my thoughts for company.

Nothing seemed real anymore.

Just as the riddle burgeoned, threatening to implode in my mind once and for all, I heard the telltale sound of Sean's imminent arrival, the noise of his tread reverberating until I swore I could actually feel the resonance.

Sean!

Once more, his approach brought with it an odd mixture of relief and trepidation. He was my only route out of this room. Whatever did or didn't transpire—whether he compelled me to marry him, whether Saul came to my rescue, or in the short term, if I wanted to eat or ever get out of this bloody seat—I needed him in a very tangible way. Then there was the obvious reality of my predicament. Sean was the same man who'd snatched me from outside my home, pumped me full of sedative, and tormented me. There was nothing sane about being eager to see a man like that.

Just when I didn't think the tension twisting inside could intensify any further, the key slid into the lock beyond the door. I'd heard the action countless times before, but still, each time it happened, my heart rate quickened, my throat drying as I tried to anticipate his next move. What mood would he be in when he opened that door? What would he want from me? Aside from the inevitable answer that he relished seeing me struggle, it was impossible to say, but knowing Sean, he wouldn't keep me waiting long.

"There she is." He threw the door open in triumph, my eyes blinking into the muted light it provided. "My bride-to-be."

A shiver ran the length of my spine at his pronouncement. Frankly, I wasn't certain I ever wanted to get married, let alone to some cocky criminal I didn't really know.

"How have you been, gorgeous, a good girl, I hope?"

"Yes, Mr. Hyland, Sir." I blew out a breath, the words he expected falling from my lips without a second thought.

Christ, what had happened to me? A few days in this anguished state and I'd ceded to his will, conditioned like an obedient pet to do his every bidding. The muscles at the apex of my thighs clenched at the debilitating thought. I loathed how he must perceive me—an easy blonde he could tie up and order around—but every time I tried to muster the energy to focus on who I really was, on the responses he deserved, Sean had an answer. An unceremonious trip over his knee for the type of humiliating spanking that left my head spinning and my arse in discomfort when he bound me to the chair again. A humbling request to demean me, often while he videoed the ordeal for so-called prosperity—he seemed to have a response for everything.

"Good girl." He moved inside the room, closing the distance between us in a few strides. "Let me look at you." One hand rose to my chin, pulling it north to meet his demanding eyes. "I have news, Hilary. News which may interest you."

My belly tightened, anxiety pinballing. Anything that interested Sean was bound to mean more trouble for me, more reasons to worry, to cry, to be chastened.

"Want to hear my news?"

I blinked up at him, knowing there was only one acceptable answer.

"Yes, please, Sir."

He lowered to his haunches, the hand at my chin grazing over my exposed breast en route to my knee. My breathing accelerated, my helplessness to prevent his exploration of my body arousing and vexing in equal measure, his sudden proximity doing nothing to assuage my apprehensions.

"It's time to get you out of here." He smiled, one side of his face eerily lit by the subdued light coming from the open doorway. "Time to clean you up. We're going on a little trip tomorrow."

"To get m-married?" I could barely get the words out, but I had to know. He'd repeatedly implied he wanted our nuptials to be as soon as possible, and despite my friendly slither of light, it was possible I'd misjudged the days, that this was it—my time was up.

"No, not yet." He chuckled, tenderly patting my knee as if I said something amusing. "Though it's good to see you're excited about the upcoming big event."

Excitement? Is that what I'd conveyed with my stammering reaction?

"This time, it's a trip to see my legal man, a few documents for my new bride to sign." He leaned closer, edging between my parted knees. "Before you get to sign the important one on the day itself."

My brow furrowed. I still couldn't believe he expected me to play along with this ludicrous plan to get married, but I knew countering him at this juncture wouldn't help my cause. It wouldn't get me out of this chair, or indeed, out of this blasted room, and from the things he said, there was a brief glimmer of hope that his plan might be a way out of here. In the end, I said the one thing I knew would please him, the only thing guaranteed to win his approval.

"Yes, Sir. Thank you."

CHAPTER 2: SEAN

As stimulating as Hilary was in my binds, she scarcely resembled the bold young woman who'd literally run into me in the coffee shop, the one who'd tipped the contents of her hot beverage all over my shirt. This version of Hilary was subdued, her pale skin absent of the cosmetics she'd so vehemently paid homage to in the past, her hair lank at her shoulders, but she was no less beautiful. There was splendor in her sunshine-deprived skin, wonder in the way she honored me with the correct title. Her confinement had helped her to blossom, preparing her, I hoped, for the vast task ahead of being my wife. Inching between her legs, I mused on the point. This woman—who I'd stolen from the streets—would soon be my spouse. It would be an adjustment for us both.

"Let's get you cleaned up." My attention shifted to the straps at her ankles, liberating them quickly before I rose to my full height and started work on her wrists. "Remember all the things you've learned over the last few days." My fingers hesitated, the pause drawing her focus where it needed to be —my face. "My expectations about how you should behave."

A small sigh met my warning before she drew her lower lip between her teeth. "Yes, Sir."

"I want to trust you, to be able to spoil you, but we have to face facts." Liberating her second wrist, I took a step back. "Right now, we have trust issues, which only time can heal."

Her blue eyes followed my hands at my hips.

"That means I want complete obedience, Hilary. You leap when I say so and bark like a dog when I order it." I watched as her breathing increased, her tempting chest rising and falling with my cautionary counsel. I wanted to clamp those glorious tits again and watch the agony on her usually flawless face when I yanked at one, then the other weighted clamp, to see her thoughts unravel when the only thing that mattered in the world was what happened to those tiny weights tugging at her nipples. My balls tightened at the tantalizing imagery. Frankly, I couldn't wait. "Understand?"

She nodded, her gaze locking with mine. "Yes, Sir, I understand."

"Come on then." I gestured for her to get out of the seat, allowing her a few seconds to stretch out her long, slender limbs after so long confined to the chair before I gave the normal command, signaling where I wanted her. "At my feet." My arousal surged at her compliance. The fabulous blonde fell to all fours before she crawled into position. "Stay with me."

I strode away, ensuring my paces were slightly shorter than usual so she could keep up. A captivating sense of joy sprinted through my veins as we approached the door, walking in my unhurried way with my gorgeous crawling bride-to-be scrambling at my feet. This was how life was supposed to be—a man in charge of his empire with a delicious submissive woman coming to heel at his side. The reality made me giddy, the kind of rush I hadn't experienced since the BDSM clubs back in Nice.

To think when I arrived in the country, I'd assumed the worst, believing the whole thing would be an ordeal until I was back on the French Riviera, but one random encounter in a coffee shop had changed all that. Now when I contemplated returning to the sunshine-laden home I'd left behind in France, it would be as a married man, with my tantalizing wife in tow. Not that Hilary would prevent me from indulging in the number of pretty French mistresses I intended to take—far from it. If I wanted other lovers, I would take them with the usual ease I conquered all things, but Hilary's roaming days were over. Glancing down at the way she scuttled at my side, I smiled. Hilary's only focus would be attending to all my needs and perhaps, if I desired it, producing an heir for the growing Hyland empire. It was a pleasing thought.

We turned the corner at the door, heading down the hallway toward the bathroom. I'd rented this penthouse from a friend of an acquaintance, and to say the décor wasn't to my taste was an understatement, but it hardly mattered. It was a base—somewhere to keep my captive until I could get a ring on her finger. Once the deed was done, I could dispense with such formalities and get us a place. I'd had my eye on a property in Knightsbridge that may fit the bill, an exclusive London address to accompany my new status, not only as a married man but leader of the Hyland empire. It would be perfect.

"In here." I paused at the bathroom doorway. The room was smaller than I'd have liked, the burnt orange furnishings like something out of a 1970s horror movie. "Climb into the bath."

I waited while she complied before turning my attention

to the essentials I'd purchased for just this moment. It was one thing to keep your woman captive in a dank, abandoned property, but one day, she would leave this place, and as my intention had always been for that day to be on the way to our wedding, it was imperative to have the basics to hand. Inside an open bag, I found two huge bath sheets, plus an array of shampoos, conditioners, and finally, a razor. Grabbing one of the towels, I flung it over the edge of the bath before returning to collect the hair products. By the time I'd placed the bottles on the rim of the tub, she was shivering in the center.

"You're cold." It was more an assertion than a question. Of course, she was cold. The bathroom was cast in shadows, and only heat had been pumped into the room where she was held. She must be freezing. "Hang on."

I reached for the taps and tugged on the hot water faucet, praying the thing would work. Holding my hand under its stream, I glanced back at the quivering woman. She was diminutive, so fragile in the face of my adversity, and God help me, she turned me on without effort. What sort of monster was aroused by a woman shaking with the cold? My lips curled at the query, the answer obvious—likely the same one who would have kept her bound naked to the chair while he went to arrange the nuptials he was obliging her to undertake. Swallowing back my glee, I was relieved to feel the water running over my digits growing warmer. Placing the plug in the hole below, I allowed warm water to fill the tub, checking the temperature as she knelt, waiting.

"Looking forward to being clean again?" I couldn't help but goad her as the bath filled, biting back the anxious expression which met my question.

"Sir?"

"I just wondered." I added a little cold water to the mix as the level rose in the tub. "Seems as though a woman like you would have been pretty high maintenance before we..." My brow rose. "Ran into each other."

Heaving, her eyes fluttered closed briefly. "I used to like to look after myself, yes, Sir."

"That's good." I cut the water supply, meeting her worried gaze. "Once we're man and wife, I'll expect you to look a certain way for me."

"What way, Sir?"

"Sit in the tub properly," I chided, waiting while she shifted onto her no doubt tender arse. "Turn around with your back to me. I'm going to wash your hair."

"You?" Her eyes widened with surprise.

"Yes, me." One brow arched at her provocative tone. "I'm going to be quite the hands-on husband."

Shrugging my expensive jacket from my shoulders, I hung it on the grubby-looking hook on the back of the door before striding back to find her just where I'd indicated. So far, so good. Grabbing the bottle of shampoo, I tackled the showerhead, wrestling it from its home and allowing the water to burst from its head. Hilary yelped as it splashed between her legs. Grinning, I checked the temperature once more before maneuvering it behind her.

"Head back," I ordered, angling the showerhead away from her as she obeyed. Running the warm water over her long tresses, I watched as her golden locks became a wet blanket of dark blonde, the water stripping the honey hue away. Hilary had just the right length hair, and I had always had a fetish for blondes.

No doubt it was torment for her to be treated this way, kept permanently stripped and bound, then treated like a child when it came to bathing, but I was absolutely in my element. Stripping her defenses away by bathing her was even more fun than I'd realized it could be, and I had the idea we would frequently engage in similar games once we were married. Flicking off the showerhead, I emptied a portion of shampoo into my palm and rubbed it into her sodden locks.

"Wh-What way will you want me to look, Sir?" Her voice was tentative as she reprised the conversation I'd started before the hair washing had begun.

"It's nothing to worry about," I reassured her, sliding my palms, slippery with the remaining shampoo, down from her shoulders and over her pert chest. She whimpered at the change of tack, her body tensing and hands rising as though she intended to bat me away, but as my flesh ran over hers, I watched her fight the urge. Hilary was a smart girl and knew what her disobedience would earn. As she forced her hands back into the water, I was almost proud.

"Very good." I crooned, relishing the way her cheeks colored at the compliment. "You're learning. What do you think would have happened if you'd tried to stop me from exploring you?"

Breath ragged, she lifted her chin to meet my insistent gaze. "You'd have been angry, Sir." Dismay danced in those blue eyes with the confession. "You'd have punished me."

"That's right." Shifting my weight, my hands paused on her nipples, clasping them between my fingers before I pinched. The flicker of pain in her eyes was bloody delicious. "I'd have come up with something dark and mesmerizing rather than focusing on preparing you for tomorrow." Releasing her buds, I ran my hands over her midriff, allowing the wrist not housing my Armani watch to plunge into the water and brush over her pussy lips.

"Oh God." She tipped her head back, close to the edge. That, I had found, was one of the blessings of keeping her perpetually aroused. It was easier and easier to push Hilary back to the brink each time I tried.

"Mmmm." I contemplated sliding a couple digits inside her but reasoned it was counterproductive. We were here to get her washed and shaven. There would be time later to goad that hungry little nub between her legs back to life.

CHAPTER 3: HILARY

Was this some sort of new torment? As if it wasn't bad enough being kept, fettered, and wanting all hours of the day, now Sean had conceived this suffering. I'd been kept here for so long—too long—I had to admit, much though I didn't want his hands all over me, didn't need him cosseting me in this most intimate way, the water was hot and cleansing, and the idea of finally being able to wash my hair and shave sent elated chills through me. As usual, he'd conceived another agonizing paradox to taunt and entice me.

"Tip your head back."

I startled at the sound of the showerhead turning on again, the rush of angry water filling the bath behind me as gingerly, I complied.

"Eyes closed."

With a deep breath, they flickered closed, my body tensing as he eased my hair back with one large palm, rinsing away the shampoo with the other. There was such trust at this moment, his actions almost affectionate as he massaged the suds away, and all the while, I remained passive, contemplating how I could get away, how I could use this bathing opportunity as a chance to flee. Of course, the short answer was there was no easy way. Sean had thought of everything, and I had little doubt every window and door to the outside world was locked, but still, the thought nagged—*I had to try*. This was the first time I'd been out of that dark cell for goodness knows how long and the only time he'd engaged me in any non-sexual way. The venture out tomorrow was my best shot at escape. I had to think, had to use my wits to outmaneuver him.

"Okay." Pressing a hand into my back, he eased me forward. "Eyes open."

Like a fool, I conformed, my stillness the very picture of complicity, not once betraying the plans hatching in my mind.

"How was that?" Once more, the showerhead was turned off, the low thrum ceasing abruptly before he came to loom over me.

"Good, thank you, Sir." I sounded like a robot. Hell, as I sat in the soothing water, I felt like one, but there was no denying it was a blessed relief to be out of that room to be clean. I was grateful for those small mercies.

"I'm assuming you condition this beautiful hair?"

I tilted my head to meet his gaze, my brows knitting. Sitting naked in a crappy old tub while the man who'd snatched me cooed over my beauty routines—surely, this was the single most peculiar conversation of my life?

"Yes, Sir."

"Just as well I planned ahead." A mischievous smile flickered on his face as he grabbed another product and waved it in front of me. My focus landed on the bottle in his grasp. It wasn't a brand I recognized, but I was hardly in a position to query him.

"Do you always bathe the women you capture, Sir?" It was a risk saying anything, let alone something so daring, but something about the look in his eyes as I turned back to him compelled me. This might be the best chance I had. Christ, the way he liked to gag me, it might be the only one.

A glimmer of amusement rose on his face, his lips—which could be so cruel but oh so tempting—curling at my audacity.

"It might surprise you to hear you're the first, Hilary." Turning the bottle upside down, he squeezed a measure of the conditioner on his palm. "The only woman I've ever wanted to marry."

The muscles between my legs clenched at his ominous tone. Had I pushed my luck by asking, and perhaps the most perplexing query of all, why on earth did he actually want to marry me? I'd met men like Sean Hyland before—far too many of them. They were a dime a dozen at The Syndicate, and I knew how their minds worked. They took what they wanted and didn't ask permission. That part, however twisted, made sense to me, but why he'd choose to legally bind us together was less easy to comprehend. If he just wanted to bed me, why hadn't he? The compromising situations he'd had me in over the last few days could easily have enabled him to claim me. I pulled in a shaky breath as that thought resonated. *He could have done, so why hadn't he?*

"Any more questions?" His arched brow conveyed how unimpressed he was at my perceived impertinence, the gesture increasing my heart rate exponentially.

"I'm sorry." Why was I apologizing, for God's sake? "I've just never…" My words dried up, his dark chuckle reverberating over me as his palms lathered the product through my head.

"Been kidnapped before?" he smirked.

"Right." Pressing my lips together, I waited as he worked the conditioner into my hair. There was something oddly comforting in the deed, as though this man who'd been the architect of such distress could somehow be my sanctuary.

"I understand." His hands paused, and my head turned back to meet his eyes. "I know it's not been easy on you, gorgeous, and I know what an utter bastard I can be. I'm not apologizing for either, but that doesn't mean I'm oblivious."

"So, you're still going to marry me?" I blew out a breath, his hardening expression reminding me of my error just in time. "Sir."

"Yes, Hilary." Lowering to his knees, he reached for the razor balanced on the edge of the tub. "We're getting married."

Catching my lip between my teeth, I fought back the wave of emotion surging within me. This wasn't right. You couldn't just take someone from the roadside and make them your wife in 21st-century Britain. It was insane.

"Don't start with the puppy dog eyes."

I sniffed, blinking away the threatening tears as I shook my head. I wouldn't cry in front of him. I had to hang on to whatever remained of my tarnished dignity with everything I had.

"Lift your arm." He clutched the razor in his fingers. "I'm going to shave you."

I should have expected as much since he'd insisted on washing my hair, but I couldn't hold back the protest as it left my lips.

"I can do it myself, Sir." I flinched at the sound of my voice, petulant even to my own ears.

"You'll do no such thing," he growled. "And if you persist in this incessant talking, you'll force me to introduce your favorite gag into bath time routines."

I gasped at the threat, well aware how serious it was.

"Now, raise your arm."

Swallowing hard, I lifted the arm nearest him, closing my eyes as he used the remaining conditioner on his hands and set to work removing the hair which had grown during my unexpected stay. Somehow, this act was far more excruciating than washing my hair. There had been tenderness in that show of devotion, but this was merely mortifying. Inhaling, I forced my eyes open, taking in the look of the faded tiles on the wall beside me.

"Better." He tugged at my flesh, pulling me this way and that as he attempted to leave me hair-free. "Now, spin around and lift the other."

Time protracted as I was forced to endure yet another undignified quantity of time while he shaved under the arm. By the time he finished, the water was almost tepid.

"Okay." He sounded pleased with himself as he cleaned the razor in the water. "Now for your legs. Turn to face the other direction again with one leg on the side of the tub." He tapped the edge nearest him as if I couldn't understand where he meant, and I reluctantly obeyed.

"Need more water?"

I met his eyes for the first time since the humiliating shave had started.

"Yes, please, Sir."

Nodding, he reached for the hot water tap, releasing it before he returned to the bottle of product and helped himself to more of the contents.

Steam rose around us as the hot torrent plunged into the bath behind me, the noise of its deluge filling my ears as he set to work on my left leg. In many ways, I marveled at his work. Efficient yet methodical, he tackled the limb with ease. I'd always assumed men would be useless at the task, given they only had to shave such a small area of their bodies, but where Sean was concerned at least, I was clearly wrong.

Handling the blade with confidence, he stripped my leg of the stubble that had accrued during my captivity, indicating to switch legs once he was satisfied. I was quiet as he tackled the second leg, hypnotized by the way he managed the mission, no longer musing on my escape as I should have been. Within moments, both legs were clean-shaven.

"How's the temperature now?" Casting me a wry smile, he shifted on his knees to turn off the faucet. "Better?"

"Much better, thank you." My answer was immediate, and as I gave it, I found I wanted to convey my gratitude. He didn't have to do any of this. He could have left me tied up in that grim, dark room, could have left my limbs a hairy, disgusting mess, and my hair unwashed. Whatever his motivations, I was appreciative that at least some of my needs had been met.

"Good." He smiled, his gaze locking with mine as he shook the blade in the water beyond my feet. "It wasn't so bad, was it?"

Heat bloomed in my face at his patronizing tone. Not for the first time, I couldn't decide if I wanted to smack his face or kiss him. The effect Sean had on me was maddening.

"No, Sir," I eventually agreed. "But I could have managed it."

He laughed, running his tongue over his teeth. "Maybe after we're married," he mused. "In truth, I quite liked the challenge. There are worse things than shaving a beautiful woman."

Gulping at the praise, my gaze lowered to the water, now lapping at my middle.

"What's more, we're not done yet. I need to shave the most important part of you."

Lifting my chin, I caught sight of his dark eyebrow cocking in that ludicrously hot way, my already blushing face flaming at his inference.

"Where, Sir?" Why was I even asking? I knew what he meant. Why was I making him say it out loud?

His lips twitched. "Perch on the edge of the tub and spread your legs. I want your pussy as smooth as your thighs."

My breathing accelerated as he articulated the task. I usually had my pubic hair neatly waxed at a local salon, leaving only the smallest line of hair. I was due for another appointment, and after all this time, I dreaded to think whether his tiny razor could contend with the challenge.

"Now, Hilary."

I leapt at his lower tone, scrambling to obey and nearly slipping as I shifted to my hands and knees. By the time I was balanced on the small ledge, back pressed against the chilly tiles, I was vulnerable and exposed in the cooling air.

"Ankles wider apart." His brows furrowed, his irritation obvious.

I had to force them wider, fighting against the instinct to snap my knees shut, to scramble past him, to get the hell out of this place—wherever it was. Pressing my weight into the cold tiles, I struggled to stay upright. I didn't dare glance down and look at the trial he'd decided to undertake, and despite the powerful stare drilling into me, I absolutely refused to meet his gaze. Alone and helpless, I waited on my captor's verdict.

CHAPTER 4: SEAN

I'd never got a proper look at Hilary when she'd been holed up in the basement of my uncle's dusty empire. Not wanting to let the ogling doctor take in the sight of her, I'd kept her scanty little panties in place and never really enjoyed the tantalizing prospect of the pussy she offered—the pussy that would soon be mine. Over the days I'd teased her, it was true I'd had plenty of time to play with her glorious sex, reveling in the feel and scent of her, but in the near-perpetual shadows, I couldn't truly appreciate the view. It was left to this moment, in this dated bathroom, which looked as if it hadn't been decorated since before the cold war, to really take in the spectacle. Her hair was a tangle of soft, dark blonde curls. Used to dating models and dancers, I much preferred a bare pussy, but even as I examined her sex, it didn't matter. I couldn't wait to get my hands on her.

"Do you usually shave?" Leaning over the edge of the bath, I grasped the blade and another palmful of product to ease through her hairs.

"Wax, Sir." Her voice wavered, the hands gripping the

edge of the bath demonstrating her discomfort, but her disquiet was not my first priority. I could tell how much she loathed having me shave her, but when I shifted to her legs, I sensed her relax, her expression softening as she watched me run the blade over the contours of her fabulous body. Now, she was rigid again, radiating tension as she struggled to comply with my wishes.

"I can get someone to wax you once we're in our own place." I smothered her pubis with product, pressing her thighs wider apart. Hilary had a beautiful body, but this was the part I wanted to explore the most—the final act of my passion for her—the only part I'd deprived myself of. I still wasn't entirely clear why I hadn't already screwed her. I'd had every opportunity, and based on her diminutive frame and the way I kept her bound, there wasn't a great deal she could have done to resist me, but I'd fought the urge. For once, I wanted something to be special, to do something right, and while I was well aware neither of us were naïve virgins, we could wait to savor that first time together on our wedding night. My balls contracted painfully, a wave of yearning crashing over me once more. Christ, if I spent too long focusing on the object of my ultimate desire, I might lose it altogether. I had to keep my head and not be distracted by her alluring pussy.

"Our own place?"

Angling the razor between her legs, I paused, glancing up to meet her wide eyes. "This is perilous work, Hilary." I threw her a wink before I continued. "If you want me to do a good job, I suggest you zip it."

She blanched, her enthralling chest rising and falling a little faster at my suggestion. "Y-Yes, Sir."

"Thank you." The blade hovered just above her sensitive skin. "Do. Not. Move."

Strained silence filled the air, stretching out around us like a web as I considered how best to begin. Just as her thighs began to tremble, I ran the blade through the product-caked hairs.

"Lovely." Smiling, I assessed the shaven path the razor had created. For a cheap disposable option, it was doing a great job. "Just like that."

Lifting it from her lips, I gently started the process again, removing another trail of hair, then another. By the time the first smattering of conditioner had been wiped away by the razor, her delectable pussy was practically bare.

"Now, for the difficult parts." My gaze rose for the first time since I'd started, taking in her terrified expression. She was utterly adorable, so susceptible to my every dark whim, and exactly how I envisioned her as my wife. "You have to trust me, Hilary. I won't hurt you. I don't damage what's mine." I had no idea if that reassured her, and frankly, I didn't care. "Now, tip your pelvis forward and help me grab some of these stubborn hairs."

She looked horrified at my suggestion but slowly eased herself forward and tilted her hips. Stretching her flesh back with my free palm, the new angle gave me just enough space to shave those hard-to-reach areas. Delving between her cheeks, I slid the blade over the stubborn hairs, and based on the gasping little mewls coming from Hilary as the blade slipped free from her flesh, she was as relieved as I was that I'd completed the task successfully.

Placing the razor down next to the shampoo bottle, I ran a finger over her shaved pussy. It wasn't a perfect job—there were still a few stray hairs hiding around her sumptuous lips—but needless to say, it was considerably better than it had been. "Beautiful."

Her lips parted at the compliment.

"Into the water now." Moving away, I watched as she slipped back into the tub, the contents lapping over her ample breasts and cuddling her middle as it steadied. "I'll bathe you again before the big day."

She stole a nervous glance at me, that delightful lower lip caught between her white teeth.

"What do you say?"

I couldn't resist goading her. I knew how Hilary felt about marrying me, she'd hardly made a secret of her repulsion of the idea, but that was irrelevant. It didn't matter how spoiled she'd been before she came into my life or the extent that moron, Morrison, had indulged her. She was mine now. She would do my bidding when I told her to and be bloody grateful about it.

Tension furled in my gut as the idea of Morrison resonated. The thought of his hands on her, his lips on her neck, his cock sliding into her sex riled me beyond reason. I'd have to live with the fact my bitterest enemy—the man who'd killed my uncle and brought me back to this dreary country—had once been her lover, but I'd never like it. Blowing out a breath, I cleared the edge of the tub and reached for the showerhead. More than *not liking it*, that mental image would become the catalyst for everything I did next.

Morrison was the impetus for the wedding—the genesis of the concept and the reason it filled me with such sweet revenge. Yes, I'd take a woman as hot as Hilary as my wife, but I would protect my interests and ensure she'd never get a penny of my assets. The true motivation for the union was her ex-lover. How I longed to be there when he heard the news, to see his face when he had to accept that which was once his, now belonged to me. Marrying Hilary was only the first step on the path of avenging Zander but a damn satisfying one.

"Thank you, Sir."

I acknowledged her correct answer with a smile, releasing the plug and draining some of the water from the tub. "Sit up now."

Wary blue eyes met mine, her brow creasing even as she complied, the confusion at my contradictory requests obvious. Why was I asking her to sit up if I was draining the water? Surely, I should be asking her to get out?

Grinning, I suppressed the rising glee at her bewilderment. She was bloody hot when she was baffled and scintillating most of the time. Reaching into my back pocket, I pulled out the handcuffs I'd been keeping for just this moment. I'd stopped in the bedroom and collected the cuffs en route to fetch her, knowing the bondage would be a useful addition right about now. Extending one hand, I halted the flow of water down the drain at the same time her gaze registered the cuffs. I didn't want all the water to drain away. There had to be a little left to keep her warm while I enjoyed myself. By the time I edged over to her arms, her breathing was ragged as she contemplated her new fate.

"Why must I be cuffed, Sir?" She was trying to suppress the panic in her tone, but it wasn't working, and each frantic word swelled my arousal further.

"Because I say so." I practically sang the words as I slid the first bracelet around her fragile wrist. She fidgeted, considering her options, as though kung-fu kicking me away and bolting for the door was a realistic choice. "Because it thrills me to see you bound, and it's been too long since I last played with you."

"Oh God." There was terror in her tone as the second cuff

locked into place. I gently pushed her chest, easing her down into what remained of the water.

"Don't worry," I soothed, taking a moment to enjoy her pebbling nipples as she squirmed against the bottom of the tub. The water lapped at the side of her face but was now the perfect level—nowhere near high enough to cause her any difficulty while I toyed with her. "All you have to do is be my good girl. Keep those hands under your arse and those knees splayed." Running a finger over the curve of her breast, I swept over her midriff and along her inner thigh, pressing down to reinforce the point.

"Sir?" Her eyes followed me as I shifted toward the showerhead, twisting the faucet until the water blasted out once more. Ensuring it was a good temperature, I started at her right knee, directing the water pressure on her skin and trailing it higher up her thigh.

"Ow!" She yelped, and instinctively, her knees starting to close, as though they could halt the showerhead's progress, but that was laughable, and she must have realized it.

"No, naughty girl." I laughed gently, drawing her right leg open again. "Keep them open, or I'll find a devious way to do it for you." Glancing her way, I made sure the point was delivered, my gaze drilling into her until that wonderful color rose in her cheeks—just the way I liked it.

Gradually, her legs fell open again, and I didn't wait for an invitation. Angling the showerhead at her lower belly, my lips curled when she cried out, writhing helplessly in the tub like a bound mermaid. By now, she'd probably worked out what was on my mind. The game so far or the glint in my eyes no doubt revealed to her where the showerhead was headed, but as I directed it lower to her glorious pussy, you'd have never known.

"Sean!" she screeched as if her life depended on it,

squirming her hips as she tried to dodge the flow of water. Her cuffed hands, forced under her delicious behind, elevated her sex to the perfect height, so she couldn't avoid the brutal stimulation. "Sir, please, stop!"

"Stop?" I feigned shock, holding the flow away as she fought to catch her breath. "Why ever would I do that, Hilary? We're only just starting to have fun."

"Owww, please!" Her body lurched into the air as the torrent tormented her again, traveling up her lips to her clit, where it paused for a few delightful seconds as she screamed, dancing that wonderful dance, the captive mermaid caught in my trap.

"That's right, baby." I smiled, redirecting the flow away from her for a moment before shooting it back over her delicate nub. "You will dance for me until you're right on the edge of reason, then you're going back to your chair."

CHAPTER 5: HILARY

"Hilary."

The voice drifted from a distant place, scarcely penetrating my deep sleep, though every time he called my name, it roused me a little further.

"Hil-ary!"

No. I wanted to call out in protest, to plead with him, insist he let me be. Sleep was what I needed, its warmth enveloping me in the protection consciousness rarely delivered anymore. Why couldn't he just leave me in peace?

Saul. In my mind, I answered him, batting him away. *Leave me alone. I need another half an hour.*

"Don't keep me waiting, naughty girl." My muscles tensed, his tone a caution. "You won't like what happens if you do."

Just like that, I was awake, eyes open and searching the shadows. It wasn't Saul speaking, that much was apparent. Saul might have enjoyed power play, but he'd never threatened me.

"We have a busy day ahead of us."

Breath quickening, I rolled to one side, eyeing the face of

the man beside me, and in an instant, it all came flooding back—every moment of my captivity crashing down like a tsunami.

Sean. It was Sean who'd stirred me, just as it was Sean who'd taken and demeaned me, but this was a first—I appeared to be in a bed and not the unforgiving chair he loved to bind me to.

"Wondering where you are?" He tilted his head, and his lips curled as if my responses were hilarious.

"Y-Yes, Sir."

"It hasn't been that long since you woke up in a bed, has it?"

A bed? My eyes widened. "I-I don't understand, Sir."

"As you were a good girl in the bath last night, I decided to indulge you." Grinning, his eyes shone. "So, I let you come to bed with me."

My brows furrowed as I tried to recall the final fragments of the night before. I remembered the horrific ordeal he'd put me through after washing and shaving me—endless torment at the hands of the showerhead he'd used it to brutalize my poor clit, though he hadn't permitted me to come. Squeezing the muscles at the apex of my thighs, I pulled in a miserable breath. The man was a monster. He'd directed that torrent at me until the pain had morphed into pleasure, until the attention aroused me, then watching my reactions, he'd waited, edging me back to the brink of hedonism and leaving me hanging there.

"Are you pleased?"

I turned my head, aware he wanted what he always wanted—gratitude for his so-called hospitality.

"Thank you, Sir," I started. "I thought I fell asleep in the chair."

Sean had taken so much from me already, I couldn't bear

the thought he was screwing with my memories as well. I had to know what had happened. I deserved that much.

"You did." He edged closer on the bed, stretched out beside me, and for the first time, I acknowledged what should have been obvious from the beginning. He was dressed and ready to leave while I was, as usual, naked. Surely, he hadn't gone to bed in his suit. "I took pity on you and brought you here." He glanced around the room before his gaze landed back on me. "I decided I wanted to hold you."

Pity? I wanted to balk—Sean didn't possess the emotion—but suppressed the response. Whatever the case, the bed was a promotion from the chair, and I would take it.

"Thank you, Sir."

"You're welcome." He reached for me, one finger grazing over my cheek, then my shoulder until it reached the duvet and rolled the cover back to reveal my bare body. "We have to go soon." His gaze drank in the sight of me. "Unfortunately, that means there's no time for you to satisfy me right now, but don't worry." Sean flashed me a smile. "You'll be busy with the task later."

Tension twisted in my tummy at his menacing tone. Although he never insisted I do anything that had actually caused me harm, performing for him and obeying his every perverted whim was a thankless and exhausting task, especially when he never let me bloody come.

"For now, we need to move, and my first job of the day is to get you ready."

"Ready, Sir?" My head whirled with confusion.

"Yes." His grin grew. "Remember where I said we were going this morning?"

Concentrating, I tried to think. Beyond the humiliating recollections of how I'd begged and pleaded with him—first to stop, then not to—there was a dim memory of the trip he referred to.

"Need help, beautiful?" His hand skimmed up the length of my body, pausing at my breast and cradling it in his giant palm.

"Yes, Sir." I hesitated, annoyed and concerned about my lack of recall. Perhaps it was all the days he'd kept me caged in this dark place. Maybe captivity like this took a mental toll.

"Okay." Caressing the underside of my breast, he locked gazes with me before clutching it firmly. "We need to see my lawyer today, which means you get day-release from this place."

Panting, I tried not to focus on the way he manhandled me, on the way it disgusted and delighted me at the same time. I needed to pay attention to what he was telling me and how I could use this visit to my advantage.

"Where is your lawyer, Sir?" I watched as he loomed over me like a dark god.

"That doesn't matter." He flashed that perfect smile, the one that had probably worked its magic on countless women before me. "What matters is we're ready when my driver arrives." His palm brushed over my teat, playing with it until it beaded under his skin. "Up you get," he purred. "I already have your breakfast ready."

"Breakfast?"

My brow creased. So far, meals had been a mortifying blend of taking tidbits from his hands and retrieving the rest with my mouth, usually from a bowl placed on the floor. A dark shiver ran along the length of my spine at the memories. Those times were denigrating but undeniably delicious. Heaven only knew why, but my body had betrayed my loathing every time he'd pushed me lower. I hated Sean for belittling me, reducing me to this wet, needy thing he could exploit and toy with, but I couldn't deny it was the truth. I came alive under his touch, and my senses heightened, waiting for whatever delightfully degrading plan he had in mind next.

"Yes."

His tone was firm as he signaled for me to leave the bed. I knew without needing to be told where to go, the place he always ordered me when I wasn't bound—the floor. Slipping from the comfort of the sheets, I crumpled to the ground, relieved it was carpeted.

"You need energy for today."

Energy? Though I might have been reassured by his caregiving, the notion I needed to be energized was less than reassuring.

"Come over here."

I lifted my chin to acknowledge the latest command, crawling slowly to where he waited.

"Don't look so concerned." Sean chuckled at my furrowing brow. "I'm not going to hurt you."

Easy for you to say. The words sang out in my head as I reached his feet. *You're not the one on your hands and knees.*

"Here." Turning, he stalked a few strides away, and I followed as my gaze drank in the tray sitting on the dresser behind him. Excitement brimmed at the thought of what might be on there. I hadn't had a proper meal for days. As though he'd just switched on my other senses, the aroma of coffee wafted past my nostrils. "Coffee." He glanced over his shoulder before lifting the pot and pouring a cup.

My God, was he offering me a cup?

"Er, yes, please, Sir."

What had come over Sean? In all the time he'd held me, he'd never offered me more than a sip of water. Thirst clawed my throat, desperate for the drink he clutched in his hands.

"Come over here, then." Pointing to the spot next to his expensive shoes, the corners of his lips curled, and my heart fell. He wanted a show. Not even this alleged luxury would be easy. "Come over here and kneel for me."

Heart pounding, I lowered my gaze, and pressing one palm into the long pile in front of me, I began my next excruciating journey.

CHAPTER 6: SEAN

No part of this gratifying exhibition was necessary. It was true, I wanted her ready for when my driver, Cole, arrived, but it wouldn't take more than a few minutes to decorate her in the attire I'd chosen. Begrudgingly, I had to admit, it was also important to feed and water her. I hadn't been good at that in recent days, and things had to improve, but even that wasn't an excuse for the game I wanted to play. It was merely for my enjoyment—the reason I demanded she crawled and waited on her knees—which was always the motivation.

"Good girl." Spinning back to the tray, I put down my cup of coffee and poured a second. "I hope you like it strong?" Chuckling, I glanced back to her expectant expression. An eager light shimmered in her eyes, evidence of how much she anticipated the hot drink. "Here."

Facing her, I held the cup over her head. "But first, let's see you dance for me."

A flash of anxiety glinted in her gaze. "Wh-What, Sir?"

"Dance." I beamed, the bewilderment on her face already making me hard. "I'd like you to dance for me. Now, I know it's not easy on your knees, but you can try. Hands behind your head, and you can swing those wonderful tits."

Her jaw dropped open, the sight so entertaining I almost dropped the cup.

"Are you serious?" She heaved in a breath as if the room was running low on air.

"Deadly." Lifting my chin, I tapped my foot. "If you want your coffee and avoid attending the meeting completely naked, I suggest you oblige me."

"I-I don't know how, Sir." Hilary's breathing was ragged, hands trembling as they rose from her side.

"Sure, you do." I laughed. "You've been demeaning yourself for me for days, gorgeous. This is just another example. So, let's see it."

I watched her arms rise, fingers lacing behind her head as she stared at me with wild eyes. Her desperation danced frantically in her appealing gaze. She wanted to fight me, to resist, but she recognized I was a man of my word. If I said she would suffer for her defiance, then she would.

"That's it." I waved the coffee under her nose, taunting her with its sweet smell, dangling the carrot she wanted so badly. "If you want it, baby, let's see you move.Shake those titties for me. Show me what's mine."

You bastard! The accusation shone in her eyes, her gaze narrowing, though she didn't dare vocalize her complaint.

"Why are you making me do this?" Dread radiated from her tone, though even as she stalled, I could tell she recognized the obvious—I *would* make her, and the longer she made me wait, the worse the outcome for her.

"We've been through this." My tone lowered, conveying how unimpressed I was with her insolence. "I'll do whatever I want with you, whenever I want." Checking my watch, my brow arched. "If you don't get those tits jiggling soon, you'll be showing them to everyone who has the good fortune to pass you this morning."

"Oh God." She hitched in a breath, and although the emotions still warred in her eyes, slowly, her hips began to move. Snaking left and right, they shifted her weight from one side to the next, forcing her chest to move in unison, and while I watched with glee, her glorious breasts danced for me.

"Very nice," I enthused, taking a sip of her coffee while I enjoyed the show. "Shake them for me."

Heat bloomed in her cheeks, but duly, she swayed her body faster, allowing momentum to do its job, sending her breasts swinging in front of her. Crouching in front of her, I placed the cup down between us and pulled my phone from my pocket. A display this fucking perfect couldn't go without a permanent record. Flicking on the camera, I recorded her, ignoring my aching balls as I zoomed in on her flawless dancing breasts. One day soon, I would slide my cock between that cleavage and come all over her waiting mouth, among many other things. I couldn't fucking wait.

"Tell me what you're doing?" I purred, narrating the insanely hot imagery.

"Sir?" Brows knitting, she paused, her incredible show temporarily halting.

"No, don't stop!" I ordered, and breathing hard, she started wiggling again, my cock hardening with each motion. "Just tell the camera what you're doing."

"Dancing for you, Sir." Her face flamed harder, her burning embarrassment the ultimate aphrodisiac to a sick prick like me.

"Whose tits are those?"

Even I could hear the joy in my voice as I demanded she admit her torrid position, and it was twisted, no doubt about that. I would cater to her every need, but she had to please me first, had to pass the array of perverted tests I laid down for her. Until then, she got nothing. Not even her cup of coffee. She could have taken the drink regardless, could have taken the initiative and attacked me, but gazing into her wide eyes, I reckoned the thought had barely crossed her mind.

Hilary wasn't trained to take on men like me. Whatever services she'd performed for Morrison hadn't prepared her for Sean Hyland and whatever onslaught he brought with him. After days of erotic torment, I had her just where I wanted her—eager and responsive to my every wicked request.

"Yours, Mr. Hyland." She gulped, closing her eyes as if the ordeal was easier if she couldn't see me—fat chance.

"Open them," I barked. "And tell me again while you swing my tits."

Hatred flickered in her gaze as she responded, the sort I was used to seeing in my adversaries, but I didn't flinch. If the woman who would soon be my wife thought she could affect me with her dirty looks, she had another thing coming. I could make her the center of my entire universe, but she'd still drop to her knees and perform for me any time I demanded it. Her elevated status as my legal spouse would change nothing about her submission.

"They're your tits, Sir." Her voice was strained, her magnificent body bared and degraded. She was utterly divine.

"Okay." Hitting pause on the recording, I slipped the device back into my pocket and gestured toward the cup on the floor by my feet. "You may stop and drink your coffee before it goes cold."

Her eyes fluttered closed as arms lowered before she clasped the small white cup.

"Thank you, Sir."

"Enjoy." I smiled, reaching for my own cup. Draining the remainder of the black liquid, I watched as she sipped hers gratefully. Relief emanated from her pores, her chest still rising and falling rapidly as she claimed her prize. "You earned it."

Her gaze flitted to mine, eyes teary as she acknowledged the truth in the statement. Had anyone ever deserved it more?

Turning back to the tray, I selected a pastry from the plate I'd already prepared while she'd been sleeping and offered it to her.

"Eat this."

There was no time for my usual demeaning style, no opportunity to break the pastry and feed it to her piece by piece. Today was about function. I had promised to be with Crane by nine, which meant ensuring we were both ready.

"Thank you, Sir." She sounded genuinely astonished as she took the baked good from me, her expression hesitant as if she expected me to whip it away again. Clearly, the woman had come to know me well during her stay. Tease and denial were some of my favorite games.

"You're welcome."

I waited in silence as she tucked into her breakfast, excitement burgeoning where there should have been guilt. The fact this was the first decent breakfast I'd offered since she'd been my guest was a disgrace, a sentiment I rarely experienced. Pride, however, was a different matter, and watching her devour the pastry swelled an unexpected vanity in me. It wouldn't be long until she was truly mine. Not just in terms of captivity, but in a legal sense, and it was the damnedest thing.

All those years I'd resisted suggestions of marriage,

dodging commitment like bullets, had led to this—to *her*—Hilary, the woman who'd crashed into my life randomly and collapsed the entire deck of cards. I ran my fingertip over the rim of my cup as she finished her breakfast, arousal seeping into my every thought, trying to throw me off course. Pulling in a determined breath, I glanced around to find the outfit I'd already chosen for Hilary. Today, of all days, I couldn't afford to be distracted by my desire.

"Good?" I already knew the answer, but it was fun to watch her weight shift on her knees and her eyes meet mine as she was forced to admit, for once, I'd given her something positive.

"Yes, Sir." She placed the empty cup into my waiting palm. "It was lovely."

"You don't realize how much you miss those simple needs until you can't have them." The comment was more contemplative than I'd intended, but the sentiment was real. Since she'd become my captive, I'd denied Hilary more than just a few cups of morning coffee.

"That's true, Sir."

"Like clothes, for example." Placing the cup down, I reached for the dress I'd chosen, spinning on my heel to find her expectant gaze. "Have you missed those?"

"Y-Yes, Sir." She swallowed at my scrutiny. "I'm not used to being naked all the time."

"It suits you." I threw her a wink as I wandered in her direction. "But you'd give my lawyer a heart attack if you arrive like that." I laughed, imagining Crane's expression if I led the nude and nubile Hilary into his office on a leash. "Best we get you dressed, just this once."

Her focus fell on the attire in my hands. "You want me to wear that, Sir?"

"Yes." I couldn't decide if she was relieved or disappointed. Stepping toward the bed, I flung the royal blue dress onto the covers. "I have a pair of beautiful shoes for you, as well."

"You do?"

That time there was genuine wonder in her eyes, and I wanted to kiss her. If Hilary was impressed with one lousy pair of strappy sandals, she would adore the lifestyle I had in store for her.

"I do." Perching on the end of the bed, I beckoned her forward with my index finger. "Today, you will look perfect."

CHAPTER 7: HILARY

He called this perfect? Glancing down at the blue skirt, which barely covered my thighs, I had to disagree. Sure, it was a good fit, and the long sleeves and sweetheart neckline were rather flattering, but the dress was so short, it looked more suitable for clubbing than a business meeting. We were going to see his legal guy, a man who, by Sean's own admission, was rather conservative, and Sean thought this was a good look? It was official—he was truly mad.

"You like it?"

I turned at his sardonic tone, my belly twisting at his arching brow and the smug visage I'd come to know and loathe.

"No need to answer." He shook his palm dismissively. "No matter. You don't get a say."

No shit. What was new about that? I hadn't had a choice about anything since the night he'd stuck me with a needle and taken me outside my home.

"It's just a little…" I pressed my lips together, trying to think of the right word. "Short, Sir."

"Short is good." His grin widened. "Especially when you're on your hands and knees."

My heart picked up its pace, the threat lingering, echoing in my head long after the sentence was finished, but there was little time to dwell on the menace.

"Come over here."

His tone was brusque, suggesting we were running out of time, and with a heavy heart, I sunk to my knees. Much though I wanted out of this bloody house, wherever it was, I didn't want to attend this meeting and had no intention of signing anything, although I had a feeling Sean would make me an offer I couldn't refuse. If the last few days were anything to go by, it wouldn't be simple. It never was. He'd turned my world upside down, and my head hadn't stopped spinning since.

"Not like that."

"Sir?" This was a first. In all the time he'd held me, he'd expected me to kneel and crawl, and painful though it was to admit, it had become almost second nature.

"On your feet." He smirked as if he couldn't believe the order, either. "Come try these on."

Gesturing toward something at his feet, my heart raced as tentatively, I rose and walked toward him. What the hell had he done to me? A few days in the darkness and I was practically excited to be on my feet, barely reminiscent of the woman who'd worked for and played with Saul Morrison.

"Sit on the bed."

He pointed to the corner of the king-sized bed where I'd awoken, and I gingerly balanced there, my attention on the shoes between us. They were more sandals than shoes, the toes covered, while the rest of the shoe opened out, secured by long straps, which I assumed wove around my ankles. Naturally, the shade of blue matched my dress to perfection.

"I'll put them on for you."

I watched, shocked, as he fell to his haunches, collecting the first sandal and slipping it on my foot. This was not what I'd expected—the man who'd detained me in such brutal conditions, fitting my footwear. I had to blink to make sure I wasn't hallucinating.

"There we go." He looked proud as he buckled the strap before moving to the second shoe. "You have beautiful slim ankles. I knew they'd suit you."

My lips parted as he worked, my brain prompting me to respond, but really, what was there to say? There was no etiquette for a situation like this, nothing in my life before this could have prepared me.

"Thank you, Mr. Hyland."

In the end, the weight of the silence coerced the words from my lips, my hands gripping the edge of the bed as he worked on the second strap.

Fleetingly, I imagined kicking him in the face with my other foot. The sandals had quite the heel, and I bet it could do some damage. My pulse quickened at the fantasy, the events playing out in my head like a movie. I could hurt him, send him flying backward and buy myself a few precious seconds. But then what? My gaze flew around the bedroom quickly. It wasn't a room I was familiar with, and I didn't even know where the front door was in this place. Chances were, by the time I tottered off on the heels and found the exit, it would be locked. I'd be trapped and in all sorts of shit with an irate Sean. Apprehension knotted in my belly, my heart hammering faster. This was the first time he'd trusted me enough to let me leave. The last thing I wanted to do was push him back into a corner where leaving me bound and gagged was his only apparent option.

"There." Smiling, he rose to his full height, towering over

me like the demented god he'd become. "Let's look at you." Thrusting a hand in my direction, his gaze drilled into me, one brow rising as I made him wait.

"You want me to stand, Sir?" It was a ridiculous thing to clarify, but after so long scampering around in the dark on my hands and knees, this seemed ludicrous.

"Yes, gorgeous." His tone was playful, but I could tell he was growing impatient. Grasping his hand, I got my bearings. It had been a while since I'd worn heels, so I wondered if I'd even be able to walk in them.

"Steady." His blue eyes flashed, a brief reminder of just how handsome he might have been if he hadn't been the man holding me hostage and compelling me into a marriage I didn't want. "Just one more thing, then you're ready." Releasing my hand, he reached into his jacket pocket, producing what looked like a thin black necklace. Eying it warily, I waited as he turned the unknown item over in his palm. "You'll wear this for me."

"What is it, Sir?" I acknowledged I might not like the answer as an unwelcome leer spread across his face, but I was fascinated. Focusing on it again, I noticed it was made of soft, supple leather, but the edges were decorated with a tiny gold chain that rose and fell from the places it was attached. Disturbing and beautiful—rather like Sean himself.

"Just something to remind you of your place." He sniggered, gesturing for me to turn around. Heart pounding, I turned to face the tray of breakfast offerings. "Hold your hair up, beautiful."

With my back to him, I was vulnerable, but I didn't dare to query the order. Reaching back, I grasped at my tresses, collecting them at the back of my head as he pressed in behind me. Trembling at the heat of his breath, my throat dried as he silently passed the unexplained item around my neck. Despite my raging apprehension about what the addition meant, it was insanely erotic to have him so close behind me. Usually, our interactions were monotonic—I knelt while he stood, I served, while he commanded—but this... this felt different. As he secured the off necklace, my eyes fluttered closed in anticipation.

"There." He tugged it gently, drawing my attention back to the room as I glanced back to meet his burning gaze. The devil glimmered in his eyes, the same nefarious glint I'd seen so many times, but this time, I was on my feet with him, dressed like he was. We were something akin to equals.

"Thank you, Sir."

"You look wonderful." One of his arms snaked around my middle, drawing me flush against his body, and even though I should have resisted the contact, should have detested being this close to the man who'd tormented me, I found I didn't want to. I liked the proximity and wanted to pant at the way his breath tickled the sensitive skin of my neck. It was almost... intimate. "Every inch my bride-to-be."

"Sir." The word escaped my lips, the guttural sound reminiscent of a groan.

"Hmmm?" His free hand traveled down my skirt, brushing beneath it and grazing a hot line up my inner thigh. By the time he'd reached my sex, I was breathless. For the first time, I truly wanted him. It wasn't just the situation that made me hot and needy, but the man instigating it. "What is it, little girl?"

Oh God. My eyes fluttered closed at his choice of vocabulary. I didn't understand why those words were so fucking hot. There should have been nothing sexy about being patronized, about being referred to as someone less than him. I wanted to ask him what would happen to me, wanted to know if he was hell-bent on this insidious plan, but with his hands at my flesh and his lips brushing my nape, it was all I could do to think straight, let alone speak.

"Are you ready to go?" He chuckled, the laughter taunting me, goading my core as if it meant something, as if he cared.

Pulling in a shaky breath, I tried to think. He was playing with me, as he always did, but the fire in his gaze stirred something deep within, something no one else had awakened before—not even Saul.

"Yes, I think so, Sir."

"Good girl." Wandering around me, he pressed me against his chest, tipping my chin to meet his gaze, and for one tantalizing moment, I thought he was going to kiss me. I yearned for it, the craving more powerful than it had a right to be. "All you need do is remember who you are and what you're there for." His fingers tightened at my chin. "Can you do that for me, gorgeous?"

"Yes." I nodded as far as his digits allowed, my mind fogging, despite the protests in my head. He wanted a docile, obedient woman—a servant, not a wife—but for some reason, those rational ideas couldn't permeate the visceral shroud that seemed to have fallen over me. "I can do that, Sir."

"Wonderful." Sean's gaze widened a fraction, his pupils dilating, pulling me deeper under his spell, and leaning closer to my face, he offered one fleeting moment of connection.

CHAPTER 8: SEAN

We traveled in silence, her lips satisfyingly still since I'd claimed them back at the house. The kiss had been fleeting, and far more gratifying caresses waited in the future, but the frantic plea in her eyes or the way she'd settled after the contact hadn't gone unnoticed. Hilary hadn't even complained when I'd slipped her wrists into cuffs in front of her.

"Are you warm enough?" I murmured, tugging her across the vast leather interior to join me.

"I'm fine, Sir." She cast her gaze to her lap, and I had the sense she was embarrassed to use the title in front of Cole. I smiled. Hilary would have to get over that concern and fast. She'd be addressing me correctly from now on, whoever was in earshot.

"No, you're not," I decided, wrapping a protective arm around her shoulder. In my enthusiasm to choose a dress for her, I'd completely overlooked the need for an outer layer. The reality was, as winter neared, she would need something going forward. "Come here."

Sighing, her shoulders fell at my insistence, but to her

credit, she leaned toward me, her honeyed tresses falling into the crook of my neck. Glancing up, I caught sight of Cole's gaze in the rearview mirror. Naturally, Zander's old driver said nothing, but the curiosity in his eyes was clear to see.

Glancing out of the window, I watched the shitty streets of the city crawl past, my attention inevitably returning to the woman snuggled at my side. I watched as her fingers laced at her lap, the cuffs ensuring her docility, though I also noted a change in her. Ever since I'd kept her caged in that room, bound to the chair and constantly denied, she'd been considerably more compliant, considerably more suitable to my means.

Closing the intercom between us and the front of the vehicle, I leaned into her.

"Are you worried?"

Hilary turned to me, her eyes wide and uncertain. Something about her palpable trepidation roused me, and not only in the normal, sick way fear always did when it shone in my victim's eyes but in a new and disturbing way. I wanted to respond to that anxiety, to hold her closer and kiss that dread away. Lifting my chin, I stared into the back seat. Why did I want to do that? Why offer comfort to the woman I'd taken without consent? I didn't care about her point of view, did I? I'd never given her a right to an opinion.

"I don't know what to expect, Sir." Tension fizzed in her voice, though I could tell she fought to contain it.

"You know what I expect from you," I teased. "What I always expect." My gaze fell over her again, hungry eyes devouring the swell of her breasts beneath her dress. There was no lingerie under that outfit, a fact that stimulated me beyond reason.

"Yes, Sir." She blew out a breath. "But I don't know what you want me to sign."

"Is that all you're worried about?" My lips twitched at her concern, such a small thing in the grand scheme. "It's nothing, just a few papers Crane needs to complete before our big day."

Her lips parted as if she intended to speak, but she closed them again, swallowing down whatever grievance had surfaced.

"And yes," I continued, already sensing where her had mind had traveled to. "I am still going ahead with that, Hilary. It *is* happening."

Her brow creased. "I still don't understand, Mr. Hyland." She shrugged under my embrace. "Why do you want me so badly? You must be able to have your pick of women."

She had a point. The Sean Hyland of old had certainly chosen any girl he wanted on his arm, but meeting Hilary had altered something. I wasn't the same man who'd landed from Nice, at least, not entirely that man.

"There's something about you." I didn't mention the major draw that she was Morrison's girl, the urge for revenge muting almost every other impulse. I might have treated her like crap, but she deserved better than that insult, and over the time I'd had her, our connection had evolved. It was about more than Morrison now. It was about the primal pull between us, the fact I couldn't get enough of her, the fiery lust constantly lapping at me, compelling my every action. I wanted Hilary in my life, and as with everything in my life, I always got what I wanted.

"I want to be your husband." My lips curled at the concession, hardly believing what I was saying. Even in my twisted world, it was quite an admission. Hyland men rarely seemed to marry, and when they did, it never ended well.

"You mean it?" She tilted her head as if she could assess

my sincerity from a new perspective. "I mean, you can't possibly love me."

Moving closer to her face, I brushed my mouth over hers.

"Don't forget your manners, little girl." I watched as a pleasing blush filled her face, the heat warming my flesh.

"I'm sorry, Sir."

"Better." Shifting in my place, I turned to face her properly, lifting one hand to caress her warm cheek. "And no, it's fair to say I don't love you, but that doesn't mean I won't look after you."

Her lip trembled.

"Doesn't mean I won't take care of your needs and make sure you're fulfilled."

Hilary's eyes closed as she absorbed the response. "And you don't care that I don't love you, Sir?"

"Love me?" I laughed at her pitiful query. "Darling, I reckon you probably hate me right about now."

Her face blanched. "It's not like that, Sir."

Frankly, I begged to differ. I'd witnessed the loathing swilling in her eyes over the last few days, and I couldn't blame her. I'd have likely reacted the same way if someone had snatched me from my life, taken away my liberty, and made unilateral choices about my future. Her reactions were perfectly normal.

"Really?" I paused, considering her expression for signs she was jesting, but her face was passive, expectant. "Well, if not, then brilliant." My hand lowered to her nape, holding her in place as I considered the woman at my side. "Maybe one day, you'll have feelings for me that are more positive. Until then, you'll be at my side and do as you're told."

Letting out a small sigh, her gaze darted over my shoulder, the intensity of my stare apparently too much for her to tolerate.

"What about me, Sir?" Her voice was a croaky whisper.

"What about you?"

"My life, my friends and family." Her eyes fluttered shut for a moment. "What about them?"

"You miss them." It was more a statement of the obvious than a question. Of course, she missed them. You couldn't just pluck someone from their dull existence and expect no repercussions. There would always be consequences for Hilary, for us both.

"Yes." Her eyes met mine, watery and imploring. "I miss them, Sir."

"I'm sorry about that." For once, there might actually have been a flicker of guilt. I had torn through her life to satiate my appetite, and though I was neither proud nor remorseful of the fact, I understood the implications well enough. Life in an organization like Zander's—*like mine*—was one long war, and women like Hilary were caught in the crossfire. "Really."

"But..." Her voice broke, and she gulped back the emotion rising inside.

"But there's nothing more I can offer on the subject," I concluded. "For the time being, at least. Maybe once we're married and the waves have settled a little, you can reach out to some of those people."

I watched as the light in her eyes dimmed, then shone brighter again when I offered a vague reason for hope.

"*Some* of those people, Hilary." I wanted to make this point crystal clear. "The ones I approve."

Blinking away her tears, her cuffed wrists rose to wipe the remnants away. "You mean, no more Saul." She tensed, deducing the obvious from my assertion. "No more friends from The Syndicate."

Stroking the back of her neck with my thumb, I pulled her closer.

"I hope it goes without saying, I don't want my wife associating with the son-of-a-bitch who murdered my uncle."

"Sean." She pressed her lips together, another gesture designed to stem the rising tide. "Please, Sir."

"What?" I wanted to chuckle at her demonstrative display. Normally, emotional women drove me crazy. I couldn't abide them, but Hilary's performances were exciting. I adored the way *I* moved her to these feelings, that I had affected her enough to produce tears. Her sobs pointed to feelings stimulated by me. "What's all this about? You're not telling me you were in love with him, are you?" I couldn't resist my sneer, undecided if I was more irate if she *was* in love with him or disappointed if not, and I couldn't use it against the bastard.

"No." She was struggling to contain her sobs, and unthinkingly, I reached into my top pocket, pulled the handkerchief from its place, and thrust it into her hands. "It's not that. It's just…" Gulping, her brow furrowed. "Everything I used to know is gone, Sir. It's a lot to take in."

"Okay." I guided her hands to her eyes, encouraging her to compose herself. Her emotion was starting to give me a headache. "So, we make a whole new life for you, gorgeous."

Christ, I was pleased I stirred such a response from the blonde, but this was getting stupid. She would make herself ill if she didn't stop.

"I have the means and contacts to make whatever you want a reality." My hand rose and trailed through her honeyed hair. "I vow to give you whatever makes you happy once you're my wife."

"So long as I do everything you ask of me." She blinked through her tears, her gaze searching for my approval.

"Precisely." I was glad she was starting to understand. "It'll be okay."

Turning, my focus landed back on the uninspiring London streets. We were nearly at Crane's offices, and my bride-to-be was a disheveled mess, her lashes wet and eyes reddened with the recent emotion.

"Will it, Sir?"

Her question jarred deep inside, and glancing back, I caught sight of her wistful countenance.

"Yes." I met her eyes, ensuring she took note of my reply. "Be a good girl, make me proud, and I swear I'll make it worth your while, Hilary."

CHAPTER 9: HILARY

I'll make it worth your while, Hilary. His voice rang in my head as he guided me inside the swanky office, the words pinballing until all I could hear was his self-righteous tone. I kept my gaze low, staring dumbly at the shoes he'd insisted I wear, rather than meet the smiling faces of the staff, but I was aware of their friendly approach, the refreshments they offered, and his replies on our behalf. I had been one of those professionals once. Not so long ago, I'd been Saul's personal assistant, as well as his lover. I'd fronted his corporate division with style and finesse, and now, I was reduced to this, a sniveling, handcuffed woman in a borrowed dress and no underwear. I shuddered at the shocking revelation.

"Still cold?"

I glanced in his direction, shaking my head. "No, Sir."

"What then?"

He sounded impatient, as if all my woes should have evaporated after one flimsy discussion in the car. True, it was the first time he'd actually spoken to me as an adult, but still

—I wasn't aligned with his plans just because he'd finally let me speak.

"I have a headache."

"Oh." His brows knitted, evidence he hadn't anticipated my reply. "I've ordered a drink for you. That should help."

"Thank you, Sir." My voice was low, humiliation intensifying as staff at the legal office flitted around us. It was bad enough I was cuffed like a common criminal and looked in a terrible state, but I wouldn't allow them to hear me speak to him like this as well. It was all too mortifying.

"This way, Mr. Hyland."

My eyes darted at the sound of a woman's voice, her disdainful expression clear as she took in the look of me. Pulling in a breath, I tensed, wishing the ground would open up and swallow me whole.

"Thank you, Polly."

Tugging my arm, Sean compelled me onward, following her to a nearby office. Suited professionals glanced up as we passed, as though he'd paid them to be here, witnessing my denigration. Jesus, this was excruciating, dozens of eyes boring into me, scrutinizing how I looked as I tiptoed past. Even though it was only a few feet to the office, it seemed as if the journey went on for an age.

"If you could wait here, I'll let you know when Mr. Crane is ready for you." The gregarious Polly drank in Sean, hips wiggling, inviting his advance.

"Perfect, thank you."

To his credit, he didn't respond to her outrageous flirting, but then, what did I care if he took her bait? I didn't want to marry the disgusting man, so I was hardly demanding monogamy. Standing in the middle of the luxurious waiting room, I watched as she flitted away, envying her position. I'd been that girl once, free to come and go as I'd wanted, yet I'd never really appreciated the liberty. It was true what they said—you never knew what you had until it was gone.

"Sit down."

I turned at the order, acknowledging he was already seated while I was still staring forlornly at the door Polly had disappeared through. With a sigh, I complied, clutching the glass of water he thrust into my bound hands.

"Drink."

This was what my life had been reduced to—a thing he could dress and order around with one-or two-word commands. My head pounded harder at the dismal thought. Slowly, I lifted the glass to my mouth and drained its contents. Whatever happened, the last thing I needed was a bloody headache on top of everything else.

"Do I have to wear the cuffs, Sir?" It was a risky strategy, pressing Sean for anything, but I figured I might as well ask the question. Perhaps he would take pity on me, my upset tweaking whatever remained of his conscience.

"Yes." His voice was stern, and I flinched at the sound. How did I inspire such a severe reaction when pretty Polly received his charming side? "And you'll be gagged for the meeting." Reaching into his inside pocket, he produced the godawful ball gag he loved to goad me with.

"Wh-What?" I'd heard what he said, but my brain couldn't process the words. He expected me not only to be cuffed through the process of signing away whatever rights remained in my possession but to be gagged as well—was he fucking joking? "Why?"

"Have you forgotten all your training?" Sean sighed theatrically, piercing me with his stare. "Have you forgotten what I expect?"

I tensed at his expression, the disappointment in his voice stinging more than it should. It shouldn't matter what he thought of me, but there was little doubt it did. His displeasure resonated through me as if it was my own. My brows furrowed at the realization. What had happened to me? Had I been so well conditioned that everything hung upon his approval?

"No, Sir." Dropping my gaze, my fingers linked on my lap.

"You haven't forgotten?" He fired the question back at me, demanding I humiliate myself further with the reply.

"No, Sir."

"What then?" Leaning closer, I could feel the weight of his gaze. "What do I expect? What do I need from you?"

Pulling in a deep breath, I steadied myself, trying to recall all the dreadful lessons he'd told me in that dark room.

"To be a good wife, Sir."

The muscles at the apex of my thighs clenched, acknowledging the conflict warring inside me. I hated that he had this power over me, loathed the man, yet at the same time, his authority was as hot as hell. I knew I was aroused by his show of dominance.

"How?" he demanded, shifting in his seat to get a better look at me. "How will you demonstrate it?"

"With obedience." I clutched the empty glass for support.

"Obedience, yes." Leaning back in his chair, he hooked one leg over the other. "And?"

"Subservience." I wanted to cry, frustration building until all I could focus on was the glass, on squeezing it until it smashed into a thousand pieces. I was like that glass—perfect as I was, yet Sean insisted on grasping me, on applying pressure until I broke into a million shards of the woman I'd once been. "And silence."

I knew the mantra well enough, having been trained to repeat it over and over on my knees in the shadows. Usually, this *training* occurred just before I was instructed to pay homage to his feet, an act I despised, but Sean seemed to adore. Naturally, like everything in this twisted world, it was designed to degrade me, to remind me of my place—at his feet, always second in line.

"So, you do remember."

Warily, I lifted my gaze to meet his eyes. "Yes, Sir."

"In which case, you know the answer to your query." His eyebrow arched in that taunting way. "You already know why you're to be gagged."

Heat bloomed in my face as he presented me with the so-called facts.

"Tell me why." Lifting his coffee to his lips, he waited, lifting his chin as I stumbled for the right words.

"Because wives do not have opinions." I was like a robot, drilled to within an inch of my life. Of course, I didn't believe a word of what I told him. I believed the best relationships were built on two equal partnerships, but that wasn't what Sean wanted to hear. Unless I gave the appropriate replies, there would be hell to pay, likely the kind of hell that involved being spanked in front of the entire legal office. My breath hitched at the horrifying idea.

"Correct." He smiled, gesturing for me to go on. "And."

"Wives support their husbands." I parroted the words. "And do as they're told."

"Very good." He drained the remainder of his espresso before placing the cup on the tiny saucer. "That is why you will be gagged. You're here to sign the necessary paperwork, not to make small talk." Rising from his chair, he clutched the gag in his right hand as he sauntered in my direction.

Looming in front of me, I could see the architect of my terror in his fingers, the straps goading as they swung before my eyes.

"Look at me."

Slowly, my gaze rose to meet his.

"You might not like my approach." He chuckled as though there was anything vaguely funny about the situation. "And I understand that, but it's irrelevant. You won't just be any wife, Hilary." His free hand stroked under my jaw. "You'll be *my* wife." Burning into me, his smoldering gaze reinforced the point. "Your behavior must be exemplary."

Blinking up at him, I realized there was no option. He was going to gag me again, force the thing between my lips and silence me whether or not I liked it. I only had one choice—I could cede and let him without a fuss or fight him, a battle I was certain to lose while drawing more attention to myself. Despondency burgeoned—it was no choice at all.

"Open up." He didn't wait for my consent, waving the damn gag in front of me with the demand. "Let's get it done."

Sean. I sent the plea with my eyes, not daring to say the word aloud. *Sean, please.* But it was hopeless, as I'd known it would be. His mind was made up, and that was the end of the matter.

With a heavy heart, my lips parted, and I sat passively as he shoved the ball between them, drawing the straps around the back of my head and securing them.

"I know you can remove the gag yourself." He took a step back to consider his handiwork. "So, let me make it clear. If you so much as touch the strap, I will hoist you over my lap and tan your hide, and I don't care who sees it." Crouching before me, his eyes widened with defiance. "Am I clear?"

Nodding my head, I glanced away sadly.

"Words." His tone was brusque as he made the unnecessary stipulation.

"Yes, Sir." I mouthed around the plastic, my breathing ragged at the appalling sound of my submission.

"Good." Satisfied, he rose to his full height, slipping one hand in his pocket.

CHAPTER 10: SEAN

Crane kept us waiting longer than I liked, but it gave me time to lay down the ground rules and ensure she was suitably gagged for the meeting. By the time Polly reemerged, Hilary's face was flaming with embarrassment, her gaze full of desperate entreaties, and my cock ached for relief, but neither of our needs were to be satiated.

"Mr. Crane is ready for you, sir." Polly smiled seductively, flicking the strands of her long dark hair back from her face as her gaze wandered to Hilary. Eyes widening, Polly acknowledged the ball now strapped into Hilary's mouth, but ever the professional, she didn't comment on the addition.

"Thank you."

Clicking my fingers, I indicated it was time for Hilary to move, and gingerly, she rose to her feet, coming to heel at my side. Frankly, it was generous of me to have permitted her a seat at all, a benefit she wouldn't be enjoying once we got into Crane's office, but she wasn't to know that yet.

"Can I get you another drink, sir?" Polly smiled as Hilary passed, her bound hand still seizing her empty glass as if her life depended on it.

"Another espresso would be lovely," I answered, sliding the glass from Hilary's fingers and passing it to the young receptionist. "But as you can see, my bride-to-be here won't be needing another."

"I completely understand, sir." Polly laughed, taking the glass from me. "Please make your way to Mr. Crane's office, and I'll bring your coffee through for you."

"Fabulous." I watched as she sashayed away. Polly had nothing on the woman I was going to capture in matrimony, but there was something about her, and I enjoyed the view as she glided from the waiting room. Turning back to my red-faced beauty, I suppressed a grin. "There's just one more thing you need to make this perfect."

Rummaging in my inside pocket, my fingers felt for the leash I'd brought along specifically for this moment. I pulled it free, relishing the expression on Hilary's face.

"This is to help you do your job well." Stepping toward her, I ran the leash through my fingers in front of her face until the metal clip slid between them. I reached for the collar already around her beautiful neck and tugged the D ring forward to connect the two. "Your job, in case you've forgotten, is to follow." I purred the words into her face as the metal slid into place, tracing my fingers back down the black leash to the waiting handle.

If I'd thought there was a blush on her face before, I must have been fooling myself. Hilary's cheeks were so red, they could have stopped traffic, but then so could Hilary. She was red hot in her tiny dress, bound hands, and gag, and the leash was the icing on her perfectly formed cake. Fleetingly, I considered filming this moment, so I could relive it, but there was little time, and I knew the closed-circuit television in Crane's office would do that for me. I would request a copy for my own perusal another time.

"Follow me." Tugging the end of the leash, I moved away, compelling Hilary to do the same. Turning out of the room, I strode off at my usual pace, glancing back at her attempt to keep up. Naturally, the heels I'd put her in weren't helping, but they made her arse look fantastic. Glimpsing around the place, I realized I wasn't the only one enjoying her performance. Men and women looked up from their desks as she passed by, smiling at her show or meeting it with wide-eyed wonder. I was willing to bet Crane's staff had never seen anything like it.

"Here we are!" I practically sang the words as we approached Crane's office, yanking on her leash when she slowed. Pausing at his door, I waited, reveling in her utter dismay as I shook my head. "Not a very graceful effort," I chided, jerking her toward me.

Her eyes were wild with the humiliation, darting left and right to see if people were still staring, which of course, they were.

"Must. Do. Better." I enunciated the words into her hair, tenderly kissing the top of her forehead. "Or you know what will happen, don't you, Hilary?" Drawing away a fraction, I propped up her chin with my free hand, ensuring there was nowhere else to look except at me—nowhere for her to hide.

"Yes, Sir." She nodded against my fingertip, her consonants wonderfully blurred as she struggled to speak around the gag, but the frantic energy in her gaze assured me she understood my meaning. If she didn't impress me, I would follow through with my threat and spank her right there in the middle of the office, then roll up the skirt of her dress and ensure her bared, spanked backside was on display for every passing set of eyes. If she let me down again, it would be no more than she deserved.

"Come then." Spinning on my heel, I eased the door to

Crane's office open and encouraged her inside. "Good morning."

"Mr. Hyland." Crane rose from his chair, peering over his spectacles at me. "Good morning."

I noticed the moment he spotted Hilary, his nostrils flaring as he took her in, yet it was his cool professional persona that won out.

"This must be Miss Mantle?"

"Yes." Tugging her forward, I positioned her in front of his desk beside one of the large chairs he'd readied for our arrival. "You'll have to excuse her, Mr. Crane. She's not able to respond properly at the moment."

"So, I see." Crane smiled wryly, his gaze dragging over her. Any other man slowly enjoying the sight of Hilary would have vexed me but not Crane. He was as inoffensive as they came and even better, a bloody good lawyer. He knew the law and how to get around it. "Please, sit down."

"I will, thanks." Wandering to the nearest seat, I relaxed into it. "But Hilary won't require a chair."

Crane's lips twitched. "As you wish." His attention turned to the pile of papers, and I took the opportunity to address the leashed woman at my side.

"Kneel." Only one word and one she must surely have been expecting, but it sent fire to my blood, swelling my already excited cock.

Inhaling through her nostrils, she lowered to one knee before settling on both, her gaze lowering as she accepted her fate.

"Is that what Hilary is here to sign?" I took the bull by the horns, gesturing toward the papers in Crane's hands.

"Yes, sir," he replied matter-of-factly, as though bound women often knelt in his office. "I think it best if you remove the cuffs for this part. I need legible signatures."

His tone was sardonic, and obligingly, I snickered in response.

"Of course," I agreed, reaching to undo her right wrist. "Don't mind our dynamic. I appreciate it's a little unorthodox, but it's what works for us."

She mewled as if she dared to have anything to say about the matter, but one glare from me soon commanded silence.

"It's not my place to judge, sir." His tone was weary, as though he had seen just about everything pass through his doors over the years. It was possible it was true. Crane was ancient and had been working with Zander since before I was born. "But I do have to speak to Miss Mantle to make sure she understands what she's signing."

His stare landed on her, the scrutiny ensuring her face burned even brighter with embarrassed shame. I beamed with pride at her discomfort. If I knew anything about the woman I'd been tormenting, she'd be incredibly aroused by the way I'd treated her. She'd detest me for it and was no doubt plotting my demise, but if I was to run a finger over her pussy lips, I suspected I'd find her soaking. It was as if the woman had no conception of what turned her on until she ran into me in the coffee shop.

"That won't be necessary," I assured Crane, releasing her wrists and dropping the cuffs to the carpet below. "I have been through this with her already. She understands."

"Be that as it may," he went on in that dreary monotonic voice, which seemed to be his trademark. "It's still my job to do so again."

"Fine," I sighed, signaling toward Hilary. "Go ahead, but first, Hilary will strip."

She turned her head, her gaze drilling into me, as Crane protested.

"There's no need for nudity, Mr. Hyland."

I wanted to laugh at how awkward this situation was for him. Evidently, Zander had lulled poor Crane into a false sense of security about the Hyland way of life. More fool him, but I wasn't making the same mistake.

"Please, Mr. Crane." I lifted my palm, guaranteeing their attention in one fell swoop. "Like your paperwork, it is necessary."

Leaning back in his chair, the older man regarded me. I could see the cogs turning in his eyes, recognition I might be an impertinent prick, but I was a rich one and his paying customer. If there was one thing Crane's office prided themselves on, it was their exceptional customer service.

"So, be it." He nodded, the only sign of his consent. "I shall continue as if she was dressed."

"I would expect no less." I smiled, turning back to the blonde trembling at my feet. "You heard me, little one. Remove the dress."

Breath ragged, her chest rose and fell, her eyes conveying how hysterical she was about the idea.

"Now, please." My tone was firm, confirming I not only intended to make sure she was naked during the rest of the meeting, but I expected her to strip herself.

Time protracted as her liberated hands reached for the hem of her dress. For one fleeting moment, she paused, and I wondered if she would try something silly like running for the door. Gazes locked, I could see her considering the attempt, her eyes flitting to the large wooden exit behind us as her knees fidgeted on the carpet.

"Hilary." I arched a brow, a reminder of the penance waiting if she delayed further, and as if the tiny gesture had broken the spell, her fingers tightened. Pulling the blue fabric, she lifted it over her head, revealing her toned body as she yanked the dress free.

"Good." Stretching out my palm, I waited for her to deposit the garment there. "Now, face the front and hands laced behind your head as you listen to Mr. Crane."

Throwing me a withering glower, she shifted toward the ancient lawyer as she lifted her hands, placing them in her hair at the back of her head.

"Miss Mantle." Crane began as if she wasn't nude and kneeling on his floor. "You understand you're here today to read and sign papers pertaining to your forthcoming marriage." Peering over his glasses, his brow rose as he considered her gagged mouth. "Perhaps you should just nod if you understand."

Sniggering at the interplay, I glanced back to Hilary, relishing the curve of her breasts and her desperate countenance, the very definition of my blushing bride-to-be—experienced enough to handle my depravity but still innocent enough to be shocked at the depths of my desire.

Hilary was flawless.

CHAPTER 11: HILARY

I wasn't listening to anything the old man was saying, couldn't focus on a single point he made. As his gaze flitted from my burning face back to the papers he clung to so avidly, all I could think about was the shame. The shame of being seen this way by someone old enough to be my grandfather, the indignity of my position, being leashed and led around as if I were nothing but chattel, and how, as he stared at me quivering on my knees, this stranger was prepared to comply. Why wasn't he querying my predicament with Sean? Why wasn't he putting a stop to things and calling the police? He was a professional, wasn't he? Didn't he owe me some duty of care?

"Hilary."

I tensed at Sean's stern tone, glancing left to find him scowling. What the hell was wrong with him now? I was the one naked and gagged, completely debased in the office of a swanky solicitor, yet he was the one with the attitude?

"Did you hear what Mr. Crane said?"

Dumbly, I nodded my agreement, even though I had no clue what he had said, and frankly, I cared even less. Mortified at my excruciating dilemma, I was rightly more concerned about the part of me that didn't want to claw Sean's eyes out, the part of me wetter and hornier than ever. Being dressed down, treated as a second-rate citizen, and humiliated was awful. I despised the eyes on me as he led me around like a dog, the pointing fingers and the giggling responses as my shame was laid bare for all of them to witness, but I also bloody loved it. A fresh swell of arousal surged at the awareness, fogging my brain until it was impossible to think. I could see Crane's lips moving, blabbering on about Sean's assets, but none of it registered beyond superficial acceptance of the lecture—another thing I had to endure.

"We'll need your signature to prove agreement on all these points." Crane pushed the paperwork across his desk. "Mr. Hyland, if you wouldn't mind showing Miss Mantle?"

"Of course." Reaching for the papers, Sean grabbed the nearest fountain pen and thrust them at me. "Hands down. You need to sign where Mr. Crane has marked an 'X' at the end of each page."

I blinked at him as he threw the pile of papers onto the floor in front of me. Did he seriously expect me to sign? I hadn't been paying attention to their significance, but no doubt there was nothing in the stack that did anything to protect my interests. No one else here was interested in those.

"Need a little reminder of what's at stake here?"

Sean's tone was sarcastic, and one glance was enough to warn me—if I didn't play ball, he would make my life a living hell. Not that he hadn't already, but apparently, he intended to do an even better job. Blowing out air through my nose, I ignored the ache in my jaw, envisioning what he would do if I refused to sign. Sean would be so angry, I didn't doubt he'd follow through with the threat he'd made, forcing me to endure a debilitating spanking in front of not only Crane but probably half his staff. Trepidation twisted in my tummy. The idea seemed unbearable, more than I could tolerate, but glancing around, was it really? I was already here, naked and on my knees, already forced to be silent.

So many of my rights had been stripped away. What difference would this one additional disgrace make? Maybe it would be worth my defiance? Perhaps whatever Crane had been driveling on about for the last few minutes was worthy of the ordeal? Sean wouldn't have dragged me here unless it had been something important. He'd been happy to leave me tied up in that godforsaken place until now, more than content to leave me suffering while he—

"Hilary."

I leapt at the volume of his voice, Sean now only inches from my face.

"There won't be any more warnings."

Glancing to meet his eyes, I noticed the way his jaw tensed as I considered my options. I wished my mouth was free, so I could have spat in his face. As it was, the best I could do was headbutt the arrogant arsehole, but my head was giddy, the ordeal taking its toll more than I wanted to admit.

"Can we skip this part?" Sean sighed, turning back to his lawyer. "I can get her to sign them later and courier them to you today."

"I'm afraid we can't proceed until Miss Mantle has signed in the relevant places." Crane's voice was matter-of-fact. "We're already bending the rules by not having her signature witnessed."

"Witnessed." Sean's brow rose. "That's a thought, Mr. Crane. This really should have witnesses." Standing, he jerked the leash still in his hand, the deed forcing my body to lurch in his direction. "Come on you." Swooping, he collected the paperwork and pen in his other hand before turning and striding away.

With little time to contemplate his action, I struggled to keep up, my hands and knees scuttling after him as he dashed toward the door. Before I had the chance to take stock, catch my breath, or decide what fate awaited me, he dragged me into the sleek hallway, calling out to passing office workers to ensure my maximum denigration.

"Ladies and gentlemen!"

I stared up at him with horrified eyes. Why was he doing this? Even as the question flew around my brain, I acknowledged the answer. He was doing it to punish me, to reprimand my hesitation, for the way I showed him up in front of Crane.

"Gather around, please." His voice was raised so loudly, no doubt the worker at the farthest desk could hear him. By the time I lifted my chin, half a dozen faces had already appeared in my line of sight, the perfectly made-up Polly one of them.

"Is there a problem, Mr. Hyland?" she asked sweetly, stepping forward. "I'm so sorry I haven't brought your coffee yet."

Sean raised his hand, flashing her a smoldering grin. "This is not your doing, Polly." His voice oozed with that warm purr he'd used on me in the past. "But I'd love that espresso once we're finished here."

"Anything I can help you with?" Her gaze fell to me, her smile widening as she took in the look of me naked and leashed.

"How kind of you to ask."

By now, another four people had arrived, pushing past the initial arrivals.

"I'll need somewhere comfortable and public to spank this one." Sean's voice whirred on, each word burning me with its humiliating sting. "Do you know of anywhere?"

"We have a common staff area," she replied as if this was a totally normal request at the offices of Crane and Crane. "Maybe that will suffice, sir."

"Show me."

Sean was moving again, following the diminutive Polly's suggestion and insisting I follow. The pressure at my neck meant it was impossible not to comply, but the fact there were multiple sets of eyes on me was excruciating. Numerous strangers, men and women, subject to my every mortifying movement. The burn of embarrassment on my cheeks, the way my breasts hung in front of me, and the awkward, clumsy way I was forced to scuttle behind on my hands and knees. I dreaded to think how I must look from behind, bent over and exposed.

Panting around the gag, I pushed the thought away, unable to tolerate the intense ignominy of the image. In my mind's eye, I contemplated rising to my feet and yanking the leash from his hands before I pulled the gag away and screamed at them all. Before I poured scorn on Sean for putting me through this and on all the others for their audacious impotency. How could they think this was okay? I hadn't agreed to this. No one would ever consent to this madness!

"Here, sir."

Up ahead, I could hear Polly's voice, and finally, Sean slowed, his unhurried pace barely manageable as I scrambled on my hands and knees behind him. Whatever happened, I would have sore palms and knees to come for some time.

"Will this work for you?"

"This is perfect." I could hear the glee in Sean's voice, an ominous sound if ever I'd heard one. "Thank you, Polly."

One sharp tug at my neck guided me to the plush carpeted area as Sean sat on an oversized leather couch.

"Last chance to sign the papers and save yourself some blushes." Waving the forms in front of me, he gripped the end of the leash tightly and laughed. "Although you're blushing a lot already, darling."

Fuck you.

I sent the message to him with one hard stare and again considered yanking the plastic from my lips and appealing to him, to any of them. What difference did it make if he was pissed off if I removed it? He was about to enact my worst nightmare and chasten me in this least private of places. He'd already stripped and led me around like a fucking animal.

"I'll take that as a no." Wrenching me forward by the leash, he pulled me to my knees, lowering his face so we were only inches apart. "Remember, you asked for this."

"Fuck you!" I snarled, or at least, I tried to, the sounds every bit as humbling as my current predicament. From somewhere behind me, a rumble of laughter echoed, the ridicule tightening the knot of apprehension in my belly. I couldn't believe this was happening, couldn't process the extent to which the disgrace was damaging, although deep down, I knew it would be. The scene Sean was creating would leave scars.

"She's a feisty one, Mr. Hyland."

I lifted my head to see a man I didn't recognize grinning down at me.

"She only needs her wings clipped." Sean's tone was determined. "And I'm just the man to do it."

"Oh, I bet." The stranger beamed, folding his arms over his chest. "Well, go right ahead. Don't let us stop you."

Sean's lips curled as he acknowledged the invitation, then as though time had sped up, he reached for me and hoisted me over his lap. Squealing around the gag, I squeezed my eyes shut, kicking my legs. This was crazy—it couldn't be happening! Why hadn't I acted earlier to stop this lunacy? Why hadn't I kicked Sean in the nuts and run away? There had been no time, just as there was little now to assess my failings. I'd done the best I could with the little I had at the time, and even in my wildest nightmares, I'd never actually expected him to go through with his cruel threat. It was awful enough he wanted to spank me in private, but to do so in front of so many complete strangers? My hands balled into fists as one of his hands pinned my legs down. This was easily the most appalling thing that had ever happened to me.

Crack!

I screeched at the first strike, not because the hurt was intolerable but because of the cheer that rose from the assembled throng. Having each swat encouraged by the maddening crowd would make this already excruciating ordeal all the more insufferable.

"We talked about this." Sean's voice rose above the excited tones of the strangers. "I told you what would happen if you didn't do… As. You. Were. Told." Punctuating each final word with a fresh smack, a round of applause broke out at my cry. "Now, look what you've done."

Swatting my right cheek hard, he forced me to wince, toes curling as the pain passed through my body. "Fuck." I spat the word around the gag, teeth clenching, biting down on the plastic.

"Now you're going to pay the price."

CHAPTER 12: SEAN

It wasn't exactly how I'd envisaged the meeting going. I'd hoped for more, for better, that she'd cede and do as I'd asked. She'd been reasonably compliant at the penthouse, the good girl I'd needed each time I'd come home, so foolishly, I'd assumed the obedience would continue once we'd left the four walls, but I'd been wrong. I'd learned the lesson and wouldn't be making the same mistake again.

"Now you discover who makes the rules, little one."

"This is fabulous!" Crane's son, Ed, clapped with enthusiasm. "So much more than I'd expected when I came to work this morning."

"I'm glad you're enjoying the show," I hissed, glancing up to meet Ed's eyes before my palm landed against her prone arse again. My balls ached as our skin collided, and I took the opportunity to caress the underside of her flesh, dipping a digit over her lips and enjoying how wet she was. Fuck, she was perfect. Loathe me she might, but her body conveyed the truth—she bloody loved the way I dominated her.

"Ummm!" she mewled, writhing over my expensive suit.

I wasn't hurting her, not really. The spanks raining

against her skin weren't hard, but I'd been willing to bet the sheer humiliation was arousing her. Hilary was into that. It had been obvious right from the beginning when I'd stripped and pleasured her in Zander's basement. She'd come alive as Johnson watched her and got even wetter when I'd dragged her through the halls half-naked. I believed her when she said she didn't know much about herself, that being snatched by me was her awakening. It pleased me, meant I was significant, that whatever happened, I wouldn't only be her husband, but a man who had changed her irrevocably.

"Is this really necessary, Mr. Hyland?" My hand paused at the sound of the senior Crane's voice, and somehow, I dragged my attention from her lustrous backside. The old man in the gray suit stood behind the throng, nose crinkling at the sight of Hilary.

"It is." Hadn't I already told him this? "I'm sending a message."

"You're distracting my entire staff." His gaze traveled around the space, narrowing at his son. The two had a fractious relationship. I'd ascertained that much from the limited experience I'd had with the firm. Clearly, Crane was proud his spawn had followed him into the family business but didn't always approve of his proclivities. It wasn't a problem I'd ever had with Zander. "This is a place of law, Mr. Hyland, of business. I can't condone this type of behavior." His stare landed back on me. "Has Miss Mantle signed the papers yet?"

Glancing at the pile of papers at my thigh, I sighed. *No, she hadn't.*

"Ready to sign yet, sweetheart?" I squeezed her left cheek lovingly. "Or do you need more encouragement?"

Twisting her body, those wild eyes locked with mine. The intensity swimming there was fierce, though I couldn't be sure what message she was trying to deliver.

"I think maybe she's ready." I smiled, peering up to meet the grins of those still assembled. "Polly, can you hold the papers for her?"

"Of course, sir." Polly teetered over on her sky-high heels, clasping the papers in front of Hilary's upturned face and presenting her with the pen. "Here we go."

"Hilary." I employed the deeper tone she usually responded so well to. "Are you going to be my good girl?"

A wave of sniggers resounded from around us, and I smiled. It was fun to punish her in front of an audience, exciting to feel their validation and know how much she despised it, how much it drove her wild with lust. Reaching around to her face, I eased the ball gag from her lips.

"Speak, Hilary," I encouraged. "Speak while you have the chance."

"I fucking hate you!" She spat the words at the paperwork, slumping over my thighs. "I fucking hate all of you."

Crouching by her face, Polly's gaze rose to meet mine, her eyes wide at Hilary's outburst.

"I know you do, darling." I stroked her lower back lovingly. She was so beautiful. I was a lucky man to be taking her as my wife—to have *and* to hold—and God knows, just as soon as I got a ring on her finger, I was going to *have* her. "But that wasn't the question. Are you going to be good and sign the papers?"

"Wh-What do they say?"

I smiled. Crane had walked her through the whole legal framework, and she hadn't heard a damn word he'd said.

"Mr. Crane." I turned to meet my lawyer's exasperated eyes. "Would you mind running Hilary through the details again?"

"Certainly." He stepped forward, slamming his palms together in one thunderous clap. Everyone in the room stopped, turning to him as if the gesture had a secret meaning only his employees knew. "I want every single person back to work."

He didn't even raise his voice, yet every one of them moved, scrambling to get back to their places. It was priceless, a masterclass in authority, and at that moment, I actually admired the wiry old man.

"Should I go, too, sir?" Polly had risen to her feet, her focus flitting between him and me.

"For now." Crane moved closer, dismissing her with a flick of his wrist. "I'll call if you're needed."

"Yes, sir." With a lingering glance in my direction, she was gone, hips wiggling as she dashed back to her desk.

"Miss Mantle." Crane sighed, peering down at her forlorn body. "Let's go through this again, shall we?" Pressing her palms into the carpet, she turned to glance at him. "This time, I'll make it the abridged version."

I laughed. The old man was starting to grow on me.

"The papers Mr. Hyland wants you to sign are standard in the circumstances."

"The c-circumstances?"

I smirked. No doubt, it was one of the most bizarre meetings of Crane's life. It was probably one of mine.

"Up you get." I hoisted her from my lap, easing her back to her knees by my side, then shrugging off my jacket, I wrapped it around her shoulders. Naturally, it was enormous on her, the fabric covering most of her chest. Glancing up at me with grateful eyes, she clasped the collar, dragging it closer to her body.

"Thank you, Sir." She offered me a furtive smile, and for a moment, a casual observer may have believed she actually liked me, that we were really in love.

"Take a seat, Mr. Crane." I patted the seat beside me. "You can go through the details again."

"Here, sir?" He peered around suspiciously as if he expected half his workforce to be waiting on my every word, but to my ego's disappointment, it wasn't the case. His impromptu chastisement had done the trick, and everyone appeared to be back in their places.

"Why not?" I shrugged. "There's nothing confidential to relay, and everyone has already enjoyed the show."

Crane's jaw tightened. "Yes," he agreed. "That much is true. Fine." Blowing out a breath, he stepped around Hilary and eased himself onto the couch. "Let me take you through this, Miss Mantle."

Settling back in my seat, I watched her take in his words, and this time, I could tell she was listening. Her chin was high, hands still clutching what little modesty my jacket offered, and from time to time, her gaze would dart to mine. It wasn't approval she sought on those occurrences... far from it. Steely scrutiny burned in her irises as she gleaned more information about the man she was set to marry.

"Any questions?" Crane sounded exhausted when he finally drew to a close. Once again, Hilary glanced in my direction.

"It sounds as if these papers basically deny me the normal rights of any wife?"

What was that in her voice—a tinge of hurt... betrayal? Her eyes were like daggers, expressing the accusation her question had thinly veiled.

"To be clear," Crane continued. "These only take effect in the event of a divorce, Miss Mantle."

Which she won't be getting—not unless I want one.

"What about death?" Her voice was quiet.

"What about death?" I clarified.

"If you die, what happens to your money?"

There was no respect in her tone, only that steely resolve I'd come to know so well.

"In the event of Mr. Hyland's death, his assets will be held in trust," Crane interjected the formal response before I had time to answer her.

"In trust?" She turned back to him. "Why in trust, Mr. Crane?" She fidgeted on her knees. "Why shouldn't I—his wife—have those assets?"

"You would have access to some of them," he corrected, glancing over his spectacles at me.

"You'd have money to live," I told her. "I would still look after you."

"How sweet." She smiled, but her tone dripped with disdain.

"I would watch your mouth, little one." I leaned forward, our faces almost grazing. "Mr. Crane might have had enough excitement for one morning, but I most certainly have not."

"It seems, Sir." She shuffled toward me on her knees. "That these documents offer me no protection at all."

"Not true," I insisted. "You'll be well looked after, Hilary."

"While we're together," she reiterated. "*While* you still want me, but not under any other circumstance."

I nodded. She'd more or less summated the purpose of the papers. I hadn't left my home in Nice to come here, fall for the first leggy blonde, and give away half of Zander's empire. I was smitten with Hilary, maybe I'd even fall in love with her, given enough time and hot sex, but I was nobody's fool.

"There *won't be* any other circumstance," I reminded her. "You're mine, and in a couple of days, you'll be my wife. Now, sign the bloody papers." Reaching for the pen where Polly had dropped it, I thrust the papers at her. "Sign now and make your afternoon a lot less strenuous than it might otherwise have been."

For a moment, she stared at me, time protracting in a silent stand-off, then, just as I thought I'd have to take drastic action, she softened. I actually acknowledged the moment it transpired, her shoulders falling before she reached for the pen.

CHAPTER 13: HILARY

So much for masterminding my escape. So much for using the time out of my dark box as an opportunity to find a way out of this neverending nightmare. All that leaving my cell had achieved was utter subjugation and the reality I'd been bared and humiliated in front of an office full of people—men and women of all pay grades, some even younger than me—who'd seen everything I had to offer. Shame burned hot in my face as the realization settled over me. What the fuck had happened? How had I allowed this to take place?

The worst, most odious matter wasn't even the sadistic prick who seemed to get his kicks from tormenting me, but the way my body betrayed me. I'd been turned on when he insisted I strip in Crane's office, and despite the embarrassment of being led out into the hallways on a fucking leash, the tightening knot at my core assured me I was crazy with lust. Sean took these dastardly deeds—cravings I couldn't even articulate in my filthiest dreams—and twisted them, making them games I had no choice but to play. My head ached from the paradox, the burden weighing heavier than his shoes, balanced snugly on the small of my back.

Inhaling, I tried to move past that, tried to ignore what was patently obvious. It was certainly clear to any of the dozens of pairs of shoes I'd seen strutting past my limited eyeline—I was still naked, gagged, and on all fours, and this time, my loving, husband-to-be was using me as a footrest while he and Crane, Jr. discussed the weather and economy. My pussy clenched as their words floated over my head, the sense I was only here to be useful in some aesthetic or functional way debilitating. Why did it feel so good to be used this way? Why was the pussy he insisted on keeping shaved so aroused by the objectification?

"I have to congratulate you, Sean." Crane's son's voice was louder. My head tilted in his direction, though the last thing I wanted to do was to catch his eye. The only decent thing about being in this position was I didn't have to make eye contact with anyone. It was the only thing keeping me sane in this torrid ordeal. "I do admire you."

Strained silence filled the air, and while I couldn't be sure, I had the sense they were both staring at me.

"You approve of my choice?" Sean's reply was sardonic. Even I knew him well enough to know he didn't give a shit what anyone else thought.

"Absolutely." Crane Jr. almost growled the response. "She's gorgeous. Where did you find her?"

"She kind of just fell into my lap." Sean chuckled. "I'm lucky that way."

"Yes, you are. Thanks for the performance earlier, by the way. The spanking was smoking hot."

He was louder, as though he was edging up his seat to get a better look at me. I hung my head, eyes closed. As if this wasn't excruciating enough, the revolting prick was moving closer. I tensed, and as if Sean could read my thoughts, he reached for me, one hand running a line down my shoulder blade, and I steadied at his touch. Even though I loathed myself for being soothed by the hand of the devil who'd done this to me, at least, he was the devil I knew.

"It wasn't for your enjoyment." Sean's tone was brusque.

"I realize that." Crane sounded more nervous. Perhaps he sensed he'd overstepped an invisible line. "I was just saying… it was an awesome show."

He paused. "Do you mind if I touch her?"

I gasped around the gag, every muscle tightening at the hideous suggestion, and for a few seconds, there was no response, a period where Sean's silence terrified me.

"I do mind." Sean sounded distinctly unimpressed. "You've already got a much better view than I might have liked."

My toes curled as the reality of the statement resonated. Crane Jr. was sitting to Sean's right, which meant he had a view of my punished backside and shaved pussy. Mortification raced through my blood, threatening to take my breath away. Of course, I knew where he was and what he could see, but to hear it spoken about so straightforwardly—suddenly, it was difficult to take in air.

"That's a shame." Even after Sean's refusal, Crane sounded smug. "I'd have loved to dip my pencil in her."

"That's enough." Sean's shoes shifted at my back, landing on the carpet at my side. "We're done here."

"Seems like you're a little sensitive, Sean." Crane Jr. laughed cruelly. "You haven't fallen for the footrest, have you?"

"Haven't you got a job to do?" Sean was on his feet beside me. "Isn't that what daddy pays you for?"

"Slick," Crane sniggered. I caught sight of him rising to his full height behind me. "Very slick, Sean."

"I'll take that as a yes." Sean tugged at the leash still connected to the leather at my neck, and I pressed myself to his leg without him needing to ask. He might be a sick twisted man, but at least I knew something about him, felt something for him. Crane's son was nothing but a leering monster. "Best you fuck off then."

"Still here, Mr. Hyland?"

I closed my eyes. The elder Crane seemed like a reasonably sensible man, though he persisted in allowing this lunacy to play out in his premises. Perhaps they were all as bad as the other?

"I was just finishing my coffee with Ed, but it seems he has to get back to work…" Sean's voice trailed away.

"Yes." Crane Sr. sounded even less impressed than Sean. "That would be nice."

"I'll get right to it, boss." Sarcasm oozed from Crane's son as he wandered around the couches to join his father. "Make sure you stay in touch, Sean. Let me know if you change your mind. I'll always have a pencil she can borrow."

"That's enough, Ed," Crane Sr. snapped. "Your paperwork is complete, Mr. Hyland. All that remains is for you to send me a copy of your marriage certificate after the ceremony."

"No problem." Sean sounded calmer. Breathing in the scent of his trouser leg, I realized I was as well. It was strange to admit I was comforted by the lunatic who'd snatched and exposed me—the same man who demanded matrimony—but as my pulse settled, I acknowledged the truth. Sean was a swine, but when it mattered, he had stepped in to protect me. It might not be much, but it meant a lot to the naked woman wrapping herself around his ankles.

"I'll make sure it's sent to you. Thank you, Mr. Crane."

Reaching down, he ran his fingers through my hair. "How are you doing down there?"

I opened my eyes to find both Crane's headed down the hall, but naturally, the ball between my lips made any real answer impossible.

"Ready to go home?"

That was an unenviable question. Crane's offices had been filled with nothing but torment and denigration, but the place he referred to as home had been scarily similar. Not sure how to respond, but certain I didn't want to piss him off again any time soon, I lifted my chin to meet his knowing gaze.

"Not sure?" He smirked down at me.

Slowly, I shook my head. "No, Sir."

I only tried to reply to appease Sean, but it was the oddest thing. As I mouthed the words around the plastic, I found the answer absurdly arousing. Yes, it was embarrassing to know he'd taken away my ability to speak, but after everything he'd put me through, Sean felt like sanctuary.

"Are you hungry?" The leer morphed into a smile, his expression almost loving as he sat down again and drew me onto his lap.

"Yes, Sir." I nodded against his chest, breathing in the spicy aroma of his cologne, a scent I was starting to enjoy. I buried my face into his shirt at the perturbing thought.

"I'll get us some takeout on the way," he told me softly, one of his large hands cradling the back of my head. "It's been something of a morning, hasn't it?"

Once again, I nodded. It was impossible to disagree. My willful refusal to sign the papers had provoked him into the awful spanking, and as though he got a taste for the public humiliation, he'd decided to hang around afterward. There probably wasn't a person in Crane's employment who hadn't seen me naked and disgraced.

"Things could have been a lot easier if you'd only signed the first time." His voice was wistful as his hand shifted to stroke the side of my heated face. "Less enjoyable perhaps, but definitely easier."

Sighing, I rested against him. He had a point. I could have made things easier on myself, but still, the argument lingered—why should I? Why shouldn't I counter him? Why not resist?

"You signed them in the end, though."

I heard the glee in his tone, the assertion proof my obstruction had achieved nothing. When push had come to shove, I'd had no choice. Weary and humiliated, I'd done whatever I had to do to make the torment stop. Even though I didn't agree with the contracts I'd put my name to or think they were fair, ultimately, I ceded.

With Sean, it always seemed to be the case.

A wave of emotion surged, rising from somewhere deep inside. It was always going to be like this, wasn't it? There was no point trying to defy him. Sean had bowled into my life, and now his word was law. Tears pricked my eyes at the demoralizing thought. I'd never been a super independent woman, but I'd enjoyed my life before this. How could I accept this was now my future—a life as Mrs. Sean Hyland.

"When are you going to learn, if you do as you're told, things will be much smoother?" He sniggered, his thumb caressing my chin before it paused, hooking beneath it and forcing my focus back to his face. "Why is it so hard?"

Embarrassed, I blinked the burgeoning tears away. Why was I crying? After everything I'd been through, why was this conversation so difficult?

"Hey." His brow furrowed. "What is it?"

What is it? Was the guy serious? Couldn't he tell *what this was?*

Tilting his head, his fingers moved to the gag and fished it out of my mouth. The ball fell to my chest, along with a humiliating line of saliva.

"Tell me."

"I'm exhausted, Sir." It wasn't a lie, just not the truth he wanted. Sean had to learn what had become so patently clear—we didn't always get what we wanted. "Just tired and hungry."

"You're sure that's all it is?" His fingers tightened at my chin.

What did he expect me to say?

"Yes, Sir."

"Okay."

"Okay?" My voice was barely a whisper.

"We're going." He rose from his seat, sweeping me into his arms as if I weighed nothing. Clutching me to his chest, he stalked from the office. "Let's get you home."

CHAPTER 14: SEAN

I watched her sleep, time slipping by as the shadows crept across the room. It was impossible to say how long I'd been here, propped up on one elbow, staring at her. At times, I was tempted to rouse her, to graze a finger along the delicious curve of her hip and see if she'd stir, but I never did. I had pressed her, pulverized her, applied so much pressure she almost broke, and now I had to fix her. At least, that's what I'd told myself after I'd brought her back from Crane's office, my papers finally signed and sealed. Everything was in place for the wedding. All I had to do was keep her and ensure we were both ready for our nuptials.

That had been a day ago, though it may well have been a lifetime. Hours spent together, holding and consoling, and unlike the prior days of taunting, teasing, and abandoning, I really was invested. I hadn't left Hilary since we'd returned from Crane and had no intention of doing so until she became Mrs. Hyland. I still hadn't let her come, despite the constant stimulation. She was as wet and as desperate as ever, but I didn't need to leave her bound to the chair for hours on end. Now, I could be here to supervise her myself.

An errant smile lit my face as I recalled the wonderful supervision I'd undertaken. I'd taken her right to the edge so many times, I could scarcely keep count, and I'd denied her, cruel bastard that I am. One thing was different, though. Reaching for her back, I finally gave in to the yearning, brushing over her soft skin to prove the point. I'd taken to having her here in my bed. When I'd first rented this place, keeping her bound in the other room had seemed fitting—a good place to start her training—but as our wedding loomed, I wanted her close, needed to know where she was, *how* she was. It had taken hours to quell her after Crane's office, and though I had zero regrets about the way I'd publicly demeaned her, I understood those incidents took their toll. With the wedding on the horizon, I needed to spend some time taking care of her, as well as making her suffer. In the shadows of this room, I'd fought to find the balance—a balance which would sustain us into married life.

"Mmmm." She roused at my touch, rolling toward me.

"Shhh," I replied, mournful to have disturbed her beauty sleep. God knew she would need it. "Go back to sleep."

"Sir?"

My cock reacted to her throaty plea as though it was the bound blonde who'd conditioned me, not the other way around. "What's wrong?"

"Nothing." My lips curled at her concern, though she couldn't see the gesture in the gloom. "I didn't mean to wake you." That was both the truth and a lie.

"Is today the day?" Trepidation trembled in her voice.

"If you mean, is today your wedding day, then yes it is, gorgeous." I chuckled at her fraught tone. Whatever transpired, I would make sure it was a day she'd never forget.

She sighed, the sound lingering in the darkness.

"Excited?" I couldn't resist playing the game with her. Taunting Hilary was too much fun.

"I'm…" She hesitated as if she couldn't find the words. "Nervous, Sir."

"You needn't be. Every detail has been taken care of, and you are going to look phenomenal." Arousal surged at the thought of the outfit I'd arranged. It wouldn't be long until I had her exactly where I wanted her, my beautiful bound bride. No doubt, she would blush again.

"I…" Once more, a pause, indicating how torn she was, her need to please me warring with whatever desire she was struggling to vocalize.

"What?" I leaned closer, encouraging her to roll onto her back in the shadows.

Blowing out another breath, she complied, her bound wrists rising as if she was in prayer.

"This just isn't exactly how I foresaw my wedding day, Sir." A tiny whimper escaped her throat. "I didn't even want to get married."

Stretching out beside her, my fingertips trailed a line over her hip, dipping at her waist en route to the swell of her breasts. She no longer tried to fight me. A part of her had accepted her fate, but her muscles tensed under my caress.

"Remember what I told you." I intended my words to be reassuring, but at the same time, she had to understand who was in charge. That wasn't going to change. If Hilary was going to flourish in the marriage, she would have to yield. "Things will be good. You'll want for nothing, and I will worship you."

She turned toward me, her eyes shining through the gloom.

"Worship me, Sir?"

"Of course." I leaned closer, tempted to take the kiss I

wanted but wary of my intensifying arousal. One more day. I had one more day to survive before she was my wife, and I could finally claim her. I could resist her lure for that long, couldn't I? "No man can love you more."

"You think this is love?"

My back straightened, though there was no trace of sarcasm in her tone.

"This is visceral." In the end, I gave her the benefit of the doubt. Nothing would be gained by getting angry with her only a few hours before we tied the knot, and truth be told, we both needed more sleep. "Whatever else this connection is, it's real, and it's strong. You can question the label, but I'm standing by my commitment to you. In a few short hours, you'll become my wife, and I dedicate myself to that cause."

"I can't believe this is happening." Her gulp was audible in the obscurity of the shadows.

She said that a lot.

"Well, it is beautiful." Defying the urge to swoop between her legs and impale her, my face lowered, my lips grazing her forehead. "You're here, you're mine, and soon, it will be official."

Her lips brushed my chin in the darkness, the unexpected show of intimacy speaking directly to my erection.

"I hope I make you happy, Sir."

My brow rose. Based on everything she'd told me and the way she'd fought and resisted me, I was surprised by the tenderness in her voice, but I didn't dispute it. Perhaps, the dream had finally been realized. Maybe the enigmatic Miss Mantle had finally succumbed to my charms, accepted I was to be her husband, and concluded she may as well revel in my attention. Smiling, I pounced, capturing her mouth and returning the affection. Our lips collided, a frenzy of passion as we took what we needed from each other.

"Sleep now." Pulling away, I fought for self-control, for the will to wait as I promised I would. "We have a big day in the morning."

Hilary

Even though it made no sense, I followed Sean's advice. I should have stayed awake, frantic about the impending doom, terrified as the dread escalated, but after he'd relented and given me the reassurance I craved, I was assuaged, my mind quiet, and soon after, sleep came. I woke some hours later, white light spilling from the blinds in the master bedroom, once more aware of the luxury the bed afforded. Not so long ago, he'd kept me chained in that awful dark place—a place where I barely knew if it was day or night, where survival was the only pressing matter. I didn't want to go back there, couldn't conceive it. No matter what the marriage represented, if it meant I could enjoy beds like this, light like this, I would take it—I had no choice.

Glancing right, Sean was fast asleep beside me. Sean fucking Hyland, the man who had ripped me from my life—I should hate him, despise the very essence of the man he was. Certainly, I loathed the things he represented and the way he did things, but taking in his handsome profile in the early morning light, I realized I didn't hate him. Sean had taken me, changed me, and a part of me accepted there was no going back, no reverting to my old life, to my job as an assistant at The Syndicate, to Saul.

I tensed at the thought of my old lover, my throat drying.

I'd thought I'd been on the brink of falling in love with him, but now I didn't know how I felt. He hadn't come for me, hadn't swooped in to rescue me the way I'd hoped. Maybe he'd given up on me, or maybe he'd never cared at all. Swallowing down that emotion, I focused on the man who would soon be my husband. I didn't love Sean, I knew that much, but even though I detested his methods, I couldn't deny I often liked his results. Sean had made me hornier than any other man, and true to his word, he hadn't tried to take me by force. Yes, he had done other awful things—demeaned me to within an inch of my life, made me pay homage to his feet in the most appallingly humiliating ways, used me as furniture, riled and insulted me—but when it came to intimacy, he'd been bizarrely respectful. He only demanded I satiate his needs when I was receptive and never forced me to engage in any sexual act. Of course, that could all change. Once he said *I do*, Sean could morph into the monster I knew he could be. That version of him could be a different matter, but I had no evidence for that hypothesis. All I knew was he'd told me he'd fuck me once we were married, and honestly, based on how wet and desperate I was, I couldn't bloody wait. I needed him—a man to make me a woman, an enormous erection to fill the lonely wet spaces his time and attention created. It was the least he could do.

Flexing my fingers, I glanced down at my bound hands. He insisted on keeping me this way, always captive and at his mercy, though half the time, I wondered if the bondage wasn't more about appealing to my pussy than my imprisonment. Over the days he'd held me, we both understood my predicament. I knew if I ran, he'd come after me, find me, and do God knew what to me. I'd accepted I was his—for the time being, at least. I'd learned how to appease him, please and satiate his needs, and much though it vexed me, I acknowledged I got off on some of the twisted shit he liked. I closed my eyes at the stark realization. I might be the victim, but I was far from innocent. How many hostages writhed in their binds, not from fear but passion? How many secretly longed for their captors to screw them senseless?

Likely, Sean had learned something about me as well. Although it pained me to accept, he'd worked out how aroused his attention made me and figured out how much I wanted his cock. He knew how little it would take to topple me. He'd had me naked and vulnerable every day of the ordeal, and in that time, he explored me and saw for himself just how horny I was. I was ashamed to admit it, but it was true. Sean had been acquiring knowledge about me at the same time I'd been trying to figure him out, and though he could never have known it when he decided to snatch me from the streets, in some ways, we were well-suited, aligned.

"Good morning." His eyes flickered open as if they could sense the weight of my stare. I blushed under the scrutiny of that knowing blue gaze.

"Good morning, Sir." It didn't feel strange referring to him that way, didn't grate as much as it had, as it should.

"Did you get some more sleep?" Smiling, he pulled me to his naked body. I went gladly, frantic for his focus in spite of myself. My brain chastised, telling me I should be mortified to seek the caress of my abductor, but my body quieted the complaint, sensing what I wanted, what I yearned for, even if my brain refused to admit it.

"Yes, Sir." Pressing my face into his chest, I snuggled against his dark hair. Sean had just the right amount, its presence soft and reassuring against his strong, toned pectorals. "Yes, I did."

"Good." One hand rose to the back of my head, cradling me the way he'd done in Crane's office after I'd fallen apart.

The memory of the excruciating things that had transpired that day was burned into my psyche for all time, yet I couldn't bring myself to hate him. Sean had instigated those things, reveled in my debasement, but he had also been the one to collect me from the floor, to hold me and wipe away my tears. In a perverse way, his tenderness had changed things, let me in, and allowed me to see the man lurking behind the monster. Sean wasn't only the one-dimensional wanker he conveyed on a daily basis. He was more—deeper, stronger, and caring. That was the man who could lull me down the aisle.

"I'm glad."

Silence bloomed between us, but not the awkward or uncomfortable type. Warm and comforting quiet filled the space. Eventually, he broke the quiet—it was always going to be him.

"Come on, gorgeous." He breathed the words into my hair. "Let's get married."

CHAPTER 15: SEAN

"Seriously, Sir?"

Her voice was etched with desperation, wide eyes pleading with me to see reason. Today was my wedding day. The last thing I wanted was reason.

Dragging my attention from my reflection in the mirror, I cast an eye over her. Kneeling in only her stockings, her hands clutched at the dress I'd bought, and her hair still wet from her recent bath. I hoped marriage didn't mean I'd take those things for granted. I wanted to always appreciate her smooth wet skin, running the water over her like some nubile nymph from a fairy tale and massaging product into her long golden locks. Those things would never get old.

"Yes, seriously." I'd intended to be firmer, but today of all days, I didn't want to be harsh. "You'll look wonderful in it."

"B-But," she started, glancing frantically over the fabric in her hands. "There's nothing to it, Sir." Our gazes locked, her baby blues tearing. "There are holes in it."

Suppressing the grin threatening to rise, I pressed my lips into a hard line.

"Only in certain places." *In all the right places.* "There's no need to worry about being warm enough. The venue is well-heated." I smiled at her uptight expression. "I've taken care of everything."

"I didn't expect this." Her head fell. "I thought I'd be dressed modestly, not on show for the whole world to see."

"You're a delight, and you're mine." I laughed as I approached her, straightening my lapels. The suit had cost a fortune. Turning back to catch sight of my image in the full-sized mirror, I decided it was worth every penny. "I want everyone to see you, admire you, and know they'll never get to have you."

"But Sean." She sounded so despondent, so close to tears, I almost overlooked the way she'd addressed me. *Almost.*

"What was that?" There was an edge to my voice, the tone I used when I wanted to frighten her.

"I'm sorry, Sir." Her response was immediate and fucking sweet. "I just…" She pulled her lip between her teeth. "Please, this is going to be dreadful."

"You're making a big deal about nothing." Perching on the edge of the bed, I beckoned with my index finger. "Come here."

With a sniff, she turned and crawled to me.

"Hand it over." I stretched out my palm, waiting as she dropped the dress onto it, then settled by my feet. My balls tightened at her show of submission. Hilary had come a long way in a short time, and her progress pleased me immensely. "Now, stand and let me help you put it on."

"Yes, Sir." She climbed to her feet with a sigh, and I joined her, rising to my full height as I lifted the white material over her head.

"Arms up."

She lifted her arms and permitted me to pull the gown over her head. Positioning her arms into the sleeves, I eased the fabric down, smoothing it as the rest of the gown fell into place. Some said it was bad luck for the groom to see the bride on the morning of the ceremony, but some fools believed any old garbage. The only luck I had faith in was the sort I created for myself. That was the energy that brought Hilary hurtling into my life, and it was the same source that would bind us together. Who needed luck when you had money, looks, and power?

"Fuck." Shaking my head, a wave of arousal crashed over me. She looked even bloody hotter than I'd imagined, and I *had* imagined. "You look incredible."

Blowing out a breath, I ran my hands over her body, my palms brushing her exposed breasts, then gliding over her covered, toned stomach to the tops of her thighs. The dress was a one-off, handmade specifically for Hilary. Designed from soft oyster-colored satin, the sleeves were long enough to keep her warm, while the skirt was perilously short, skimming the tops of her pearl stockings. The most advantageous aspect of the design, though, was the top of the middle section. Above the corset style center, the dress was cut away, thin panels rising to form the pretty neckline, leaving her amazing assets on show. I grinned at how right I'd been about the design, my idea from the get-go.

"Sir." She swallowed, briefly gazing down at her bared breasts. "I can't get married like this."

"Of course, you can." I beamed as I caught her chin between my thumb and forefinger. "This is precisely how you'll say *I do*. It's how I want you."

Her brows furrowed, and for a moment, I thought she was going to argue, but one hard stare ended that strategy.

"Don't worry," I cooed. "You're amazing."

"I look like a cheap whore," she grumbled.

"Correction." My digits tightened on her flesh. "You're *my* cheap whore, and I'll fucking kill anyone else who tells you that's how you look." Winking at her, I threw her my most devastating smile. "Understand?"

"Yes, Sir."

I could see how much she despised the dress, how it would kill her to have to wear it, but poor little Hilary didn't know the half of it. "Let me brush your hair before it dries." I grabbed the hairbrush from the nearby counter and started work on her tresses.

"I'm not much of a hairdresser, I'm afraid." Chuckling, I ran the bristles through her hair. She was so beautiful. "I could have paid to have one here, but I thought you'd prefer the personal touch."

"It's fine, Sir." She sighed, clearly still coming to terms with my choice of attire.

"You'll wear it down," I told her, enjoying the way I got to make all the decisions. Most women planned their special day down to every minute detail, but Hilary had left all that to me—she'd had no choice. "If it bothers you later, I'll tie it back for you." I was, after all, exceptionally experienced at bonds and knots. Guiding her toward the mirror, I presented her with the wonderful reality.

"See how gorgeous you are?"

"Oh God." Her eyes widened as she took in how exquisite she looked.

"Exactly." Leaning forward, I pulled her hair to one side and kissed the side of her neck. "I'm going to have a perpetual hard-on all fucking day." Her gaze flitted to mine, my arms snaking around her middle as I pushed my excitement against her. "See?"

"Yes, Sir." Her tone was husky, but I couldn't tell if arousal or apprehension inspired the response. Not that it mattered.

I knew my hot little blonde well enough to know she'd be wet and desperate for me before too long.

"Now for the final touches."

She tensed when I left her, turning to follow me with her gaze as I wandered to the dresser. Collecting the white collar I'd had made for this precise moment, I selected the appropriate box of shoes and made my way back to her.

"Here." I placed the shoebox by her feet. "You can put those on, but first, let me adorn you."

Her breath was ragged as she eyed the collar, the twenty-four-carat gold piece entwined with satin, matching her dress. Naturally, it had a D ring embedded in the front, a sign of my intentions for my bride.

"Hold still." Draping it around her neck, I drew the clasp at her nape, locking it in place with a kiss. "Put on your shoes and show me how you look."

Of course, it was insanity to even question what was patently obvious. Hilary was my every fucking wet dream in one stunning reality. Stalking to the counter, I snatched the champagne I had waiting on ice while we dressed, lifting it from the container as I eased the cork away. I turned in time to see her fiddling with the first shoe, every inch Cinderella as she balanced on the vanity stool, sliding her stocking-clad foot into the off-white sandal. She glanced up as the cork burst from the bottle, meeting my eyes before I focused on ensuring some of the alcohol was directed into the waiting flutes.

"Here." Dropping the bottle back into the ice bucket, I collected both glasses and sauntered back to my bride-to-be. She was securing the second sandal as I approached. "Let me look at you."

Nibbling her lower lip, she glanced up nervously, though

why she was insecure was anybody's guess. Hilary was hot as hell.

"Turn around," I ordered, lifting one flute to my lips and taking a sip as she obeyed. Teetering on her new heels, she rotated clockwise, giving me a fabulous view of her barely-covered arse before she swiveled back to face me.

"Wonderful." I handed her the other flute, clinking it with my own before I took a step back and admired her. "To you, my love."

"Your love?" Clutching the champagne, anxious eyes met mine.

"A figure of speech, Hilary." I shrugged, my lips curling at how self-conscious she was about her bared breasts. She tried to cover them with her sleeves but only succeeded in pushing the astonishing assets together in a gratuitous, curvaceous display. "And stop doing that." I laughed, compelling her arms to her side. "Or I'll be forced to tie your wrists behind your back, then you won't be able to enjoy your drink."

Her chin fell at the criticism, but her nipples hardened at my tone. She wouldn't be able to hide their reactions from anyone today.

"As I was saying." Edging toward her, I lifted her glass toward her lips. "To you."

"Thank you, Sir." Her voice was loaded with emotion as she received the toast, sipping the bubbles in her glass.

"You're the most beautiful bride," I assured her. "Our guests will be talking about you for years to come."

Her face blanched. "That's what I'm worried about, Sir."

"No need to worry." Her responses were both amusing and downright scintillating. "This is precisely how I envisaged our day. You'll be the center of everything, and once we say I do, I'll finally be able to get my hands on you properly."

"Are you going to fuck me, Sir?" Her gaze flitted to my face.

"Oh, yes." Taking a step closer, I pressed against her, my jacket skimming her exposed chest. "I'm going to do incredibly bad things to you."

"Bad things, Sir?" She blinked, her amazing chest rising and falling at the certainty in my voice.

"Deliciously wicked," I enunciated, relishing the way her face heated as she registered them. "You like the sound of that, don't you, Hilary?"

"Yes, Sir." There wasn't a flicker of hesitation from her now. "I'm so desperate for you."

"That's what comes of all those hours of denial, gorgeous." Snickering, I tucked the loose strands of her hair behind her ear. "All those times you've been left wanting while I've come all over you or down that lush throat." I grinned at the memories. "Today, that all ends. Today, we both get pleasure."

She gasped, eyeing my lips as if she was considering stealing a kiss.

"Today, I get to fuck you… 'til death do us part."

CHAPTER 16: HILARY

I'd never been one of those girls who dreamed of her wedding day, never fantasized about horse-drawn carriages and white dresses, but if I was asked—before all of this torrid torment—I had a vague idea what I'd have liked. A sleek black Rolls Royce perhaps, taking me to the church or a country house for the wedding reception. Never in my darkest dreams would I have pictured this, being trussed in this awful dress—if that's what you could call it—leashed with a freaking lead which matched my outfit and led around like a humiliated puppy dog.

"Get in the car," Sean growled in my ear, brushing up behind me as his hands reached for my breasts, tugging at my vulnerable nipples.

Groaning, I arched my back, eyes fluttering closed as I tried to think. I wanted to bat his hands away, to stop him from drawing attention to my bared chest, but that was stupid. As if the men falling over themselves to open the door to his limousine hadn't already spotted his half-naked bride. As if they hadn't already ogled me. I knew it was just the beginning. I had no idea where we were headed or who would be there, but one thing was guaranteed. Sean had designed the entire day, so I would be observed and scrutinized. Not that I could have batted his hands away. Sean had put pay to that ability after I'd finished my glass of bubbles, dragging my wrists to the small of my back and securing them with some white ribbon. As ever, the man had an answer to everything.

He marched me down to the basement of the place where I'd been held, just as he'd done when we visited Crane's office. The long, luxury car was waiting, a selection of his men making themselves look busy as we neared.

"Good morning, Mr. Hyland." The same driver who'd taken us to Crane waited at the driver's door, averting his eyes from my scantily-clad approach.

"Good morning, Cole."

Sean was practically beaming. Exposing me this way for nothing but his own amusement, he was happier than I'd seen him when I'd got down on my knees and kissed his feet in the morning, brighter than he'd been after most blow jobs. Heart pounding, I allowed him to guide me into the car, slipping in beside me before Cole closed the door. At least I hadn't been subjected to those horrendous ordeals this morning. It was something of a reprieve. Paying homage to him in the usual denigrating way, coupled with this so-called wedding gown, might have been too much.

"Are you excited?" Turning to me, he reached across the interior and grasped the sleeve of my dress.

"Still a little nervous, Sir," I whispered, glancing the other way as Cole took his place behind the wheel. I was glad to be in the comparative sanctuary of the car but all too aware Sean's driver could look at me whenever he wanted. Frustrated arousal bloomed, and I pressed my thighs together, squirming against the black leather seat.

"Nervous or horny?" Sean fixed me with a stare, his lips curling as if he already knew the answer. "Does my little bride-to-be enjoy being the center of attention?" He eased across the seat toward me as I shook my head.

"No, Sir," I insisted. "No, I loathe it."

"Let me check." He arched an eyebrow, patting his lap in clarification. "Get over my lap now and let me check."

"Sir?" I managed to stretch the word into three syllables, my gaze flitting to Cole. His attention might be on the road, but if Sean got his way, we might be offering a tempting distraction.

"Over my lap." His terse tone told me in no uncertain terms how he felt about being made to wait. Heart racing, I edged across the seat toward him.

"Please," I implored him, although I didn't know why. In all the time he'd held me captive, Sean had rarely shown mercy and never listened to my opinion, but still, all I could do was beg and hope. "Sir, not here."

"Yes, here."

Tugging on the leash still connected to the collar at my neck, he jerked me forward, catching me as I stumbled and guided me down over him. In the end, I went without a fight. With my hands tied behind me, it was perilous enough being manhandled while we were on the move. I didn't want to end up in the footwell for good measure.

"That's better."

Face pressed into the leather, I gasped for breath as his hands moved over my body, edging up the obscenely small skirt and dipping between my legs. Of course, I was dripping with need. I was always horny.

"Lovely." I could hear the smile on his face. "Just as I suspected. You're ready for me."

"Oh God." Heat bloomed in my face as he explained the obvious to anyone who cared to listen.

"Time for this."

I tensed at his words, twisting to see him rummage in his jacket pocket. I froze in panic—nothing positive was ever produced from Sean's pockets.

"Nothing to worry about," he assured me, holding up a small white butt plug. I clenched, a wave of terror crashing over me as I realized what he had in mind. "Just a little something I bought for you. Arse in the air."

Lifting his left leg, he forced my hips up as he dipped the end of the plug along my wet seam. The threatened intrusion and its cold temperature were more shocking than the sensation itself. I actually enjoyed anal sex but hadn't planned to be plugged on my wedding day.

"Beautiful," he mused. "So good of you to lubricate it for me." Splaying my cheeks with his free hand, he dragged the plug along my body, nudging at the hole he wanted to fill.

"Please." I was fraught, not because I didn't want the plug, but because, like everything else, I had no choice. Fettered and over his knee, I was being plugged while en route to a wedding I'd never agreed to. It was completely maddening.

"Relax. It will be better if you relax, but you know it's going in, regardless."

Fuck. Tensing, I fought my body's instinctive response, compelling myself to breathe and open up for him, but it wasn't easy. Sean had blown into my life like a tornado, making demands and compelling compliance. This humiliation was only the latest in a long line.

"Breathe, beautiful."

Squeezing my eyes closed, I pulled in a deep breath, filling my lungs with air before gradually releasing it.

"Good." He tapped my exposed cheek. "Again."

Knowing what my resistance would earn me, I drew in another breath before slowly letting the air go. He struck, and the end of the plug, lubricated with my arousal, slipped inside my rectum. By the time I acknowledged the intrusion, tensing around it, it was too late. Sean had pushed it inside me. I gasped at the abrupt sensation as it slotted into place.

"Gorgeous." Patting the end of the plug, his dark laughter filled the interior of the car. "And just so you're aware, there's a pretty little flower at the base for everyone to enjoy."

Great. I heaved in a breath, my lips grazing the leather seat as I tried to acclimatize to the plug.

"What do you say?"

I wanted to roll my eyes. Did he seriously expect me to express gratitude for the way he'd spruced me up like a turkey at Christmas? This was Sean Hyland—of course, he did.

"Thank you, Sir."

It was easier to play the role of grateful submissive face-first over his lap, but still, the idea jarred me, goading what had once been my self-esteem. I didn't deserve this. I was worth more than this. Yet the thought lingered—if that was true, why was I so affected by the treatment? Why did I secretly crave more of it?

"Up you go."

His tone was unemotional as he righted me, easing me back to a seated position at his left side. Clenching and squirming against the latest addition to my perverted ensemble, I glanced at him, and at that moment, it all fell into place. This was who Sean was—a dispassionate bastard who thought nothing of demeaning and exhibiting me in front of his leering friends. This was the man who'd taken me, the one who'd bullied me into marriage.

Blinking away the well of frustrated fear threatening to

rise, I turned away, my gaze scanning the outside world as it raced by. He was also the man who'd moved me, stirred things in my soul I hadn't even known existed. This was all so messed up, I was never going to be able to reconcile it.

How could I have been so stupid to be abducted? Me, of all people, with all the connections and experiences I had working with The Syndicate? And speaking of my old friends, where the hell were they when I needed them? Evidently, Saul hadn't cared for me at all if he could leave me to rot with Hyland. He must know what fate had befallen me by now, yet in all the days I'd been held, he'd never come—no one had.

I was on my own.

"Hilary."

I jumped at Sean's voice, the weight of my woe so heavy, I'd been completely lost in my thoughts.

"It's okay." He leaned closer, turning toward me as one hand rose to my face. I closed my eyes tightly, an instinctive response to his looming palm, but to my surprise, it wasn't pain that greeted me but the gentle caress of his fingertips. "I know this is a lot."

That was the fucking underestimate of the millennium.

"I understand."

Fighting for composure, I blinked my eyes open, wishing I could wipe my tears away, but with my hands tethered, that was impossible.

"Here." Concerned blue eyes flashed as his fingers rose and dabbed the tears away. "You'll be okay. We're going to do this, and you're going to be adored. Once you're legally married, I promise I'll give you everything you've been denied the last few days."

His warm breath washed over me as that tantalizing brow

arched. I knew precisely what he referred to, and my pussy clenched at the promise.

"I'm scared."

There seemed no harm admitting it. What did I have to lose? I was already on my way to my fate, about to become Mrs. Sean Hyland, whether I wanted to or not, but the worst was, deep down, I didn't know. Sean had opened doors no one else had ever found. He knew me, could play my body like an instrument. If he learned to ease up on the constant subjugation, it wouldn't be all bad being his wife. Maybe I would survive, flourish even?

"I know." His voice was tender as he stroked the side of my face. "You're a smart woman, Hilary. That's one of the many reasons I want you so much. You know what's at stake today."

"Yes, Sir." I nodded against his palm—the same hand which had spanked me, the same one that had teased and denied.

"Just keep being my good girl, and things will be fine." His lips curled as if some devilish plan was unraveling in his head. Unease churned. I still had no clue where we were going or what he had planned for our wedding day. "Get through today, and I will reward you."

Get through? The words resounded in my mind, far from reassuring.

Pressing himself against my breasts, one hand reached down, grabbing my behind while the other rose into my hair.

"Any questions?"

Was he serious? I had a thousand questions, none of which he wanted to hear, and fewer still, he was likely to answer.

"More of a request, Sir." In the end, none of my queries were sufficient, but one concern demanded clarity.

"A request?" His brow rose as though he couldn't believe my audacity. "Go on then. I'm feeling generous."

Pulling in air, I steeled myself.

"I know you like to show me off." Fresh embarrassment heated my face, a hundred reminiscences rushing to my mind of how I'd been exposed and degraded.

"I do." He grinned, no doubt musing on the same memories.

"But please, Sir, don't let anyone else touch me, or…." My voice trailed away, my throat drying as I considered how best to explain myself.

"You don't have to worry on that score." His expression hardened. "I'll display you as I see fit because it makes me hard, and I know you secretly love it, but no one else is ever going to have you again." Fire burned in his eyes with the vow. "Want to know why?"

I wasn't sure I did, but I was so engrossed in his captivating gaze that it was easier just to acquiesce.

"Yes, Sir."

"Because you're mine." His mouth grazed over mine, his lips hot as they teased. "And no one touches what belongs to me."

CHAPTER 17: SEAN

Arriving at the church, I glanced at the gray sky. St. Felix had been my parish once, the place I was baptized and received my first communion. It was the only place I could contemplate taking my marriage vows, and fortunately for me, the local priest was a close family friend and someone who knew and accepted my family's darker proclivities. I'd run the outline of the ceremony past him a few days ago and received nothing but praise for my commitment to the Bible. The Good Book told women to submit to their husbands, which wasn't going to be a problem as far as my marriage went.

"Church?" Gazing out of the opposite window, Hilary turned to me with wide eyes. "We're getting married in a church?"

"Of course." I smiled, amused at her shock and still completely floored by how fucking hot she looked. "What did you expect? There is only one way of doing this properly."

"I..." She paused. "I just didn't think a clergyman would approve of my attire."

"Perhaps not all of them," I concurred, reaching forward to tweak the nipple nearest me. "But Father Joseph is a friend of my family and understands my needs."

"Oh."

At that moment, the door opened. Cole was waiting to offer me a smile.

"Ready, sir?"

Straightening, I nodded to him.

I was ready—ready to make Hilary my wife, ready to seal the deal in the eyes of God, and ready to smear the reality in Morrison's face.

"Yes." Stepping out of the car, I adjusted my bow tie. "Please make sure Miss Mantle follows me in."

Cole smiled. "Yes, sir. Will she have someone giving her away?"

I turned at the question, my gaze landing on the blonde waiting to be mine. The leash I'd attached to her collar hung between her protruding breasts, and her face was almost as red as her fabulous arse was going to be once she was my wife. It was funny, but in all the time I'd detained her, I'd never even asked about her family, her wishes, or who she might like to attend. None of that mattered. No one was coming except those I trusted. The guest list was non-negotiable.

"Hilary will be walking herself down the aisle." My lips twitched, imagining the scintillating view. "My men have instructions about security once she's inside."

"Very good, sir."

Crouching down to get one last look at her, I offered what I hoped was a reassuring smile.

"See you inside, beautiful. Don't keep me waiting."

Closing the door, I met Cole's gaze. "I'm relying on you to

make sure she doesn't do anything stupid. Not that she could get far in those heels, but... you know what I mean."

"I do indeed, sir." Cole grinned. "You can rely on me."

"Good." With a glance back at the enormous car which had ferried us to the church, I lifted my chin to the sky as I wandered inside. The clouds were still heavy, but if I didn't know better, it seemed as though they were thinning, as if the sun might break through at any moment.

Hilary

Fidgeting on the vast back seat all alone, I considered my options. With my hands bound behind me, there wasn't much I could do to get out of the car. I'd need Sean's driver to help me, and until then, I was trapped, like a lamb waiting for slaughter. Apprehension knotted, blossoming into tension that tore at me, demanding an answer—*what was my plan?* How was I going to get out of this? Even as I fought to catch my breath, I knew the likely retort. I wasn't getting out of this. Any hope I had of avoiding my date with destiny had been cast aside when he put me in these fetters and bloody heels. It had been hard enough making it to the car with Sean's help. God only knew how I would make it anywhere else.

Peering past the darkened glass, I could just make out the entrance to the huge church. A church? I shook my head. How could any man of God condone a union like this? We hadn't even met with him, hadn't undertaken any of the normal processes which would allow a church wedding, but then, this was Sean Hyland. A man like him could veto just about any rule or regulation. No doubt a generous donation to the church had lubricated the wheels of the deal. My muscles tightened around the plug, which had been unceremoniously shoved inside me.

This couldn't be happening, could it? I wasn't really about to make the most important commitment of my life in front of a pervert priest while topless with a butt plug wedged between my arse cheeks.

The door opened at my side, the gust of cool air attacking my exposed breasts.

"Miss Mantle." Cole averted his eyes as he waited for me. He was about the only gentleman on Sean's payroll, though still not gentleman enough to see reason and let me go. "Mr. Hyland has asked me to help you into the church."

"Thank you." It was excruciating, having to respond politely when I was half-naked and so damn vulnerable. At that moment, I decided to seize the moment. It was the last chance I'd have before Sean got his way. "Can you help me?"

Cole's eyes flitted to my face. "Certainly, Miss." Leaning down, he reached for my arm as I slid my feet onto the gravel below and hobbled out of the vehicle. Tugging down the back of my dress with my bound hands, I waited as he closed the door.

"Can you help me get away from here?" My heart hammered in my chest with the plea. "Please, I can't go through with this. I can't marry him. Just look at me!"

Adhering to my request, his gaze traveled down my chest. "Your wedding gown is certainly not traditional, Miss," he agreed. "But it's Mr. Hyland's choice."

"Why don't I get a say?" It was ridiculous. I was like a petulant child, weight shifting from one foot to the other as I made my case to the driver, the only hope I had—my last opportunity for freedom beyond Hyland.

Edging toward me, he smiled sympathetically. "Mr. Hyland's word is law, Miss." His brow rose as if imploring me to see reason. "Every one of us has to understand that. So, while I have compassion for you, there's absolutely no way I will go against his orders."

"Please." I was on the verge of tears again, a gust of cold wind almost taking my breath away.

"Come now." Wandering to my side, he guided me in the direction of the church. "I know he can be severe, but he's no ogre."

That was a matter of opinion.

"And between you and me, Miss." Cole leaned closer, whispering the words into my ear. "The young Mr. Hyland is a lot more respectful to women than his late uncle, God rest his soul."

"*More* respectful?" I turned to meet his eyes.

"Yes," he confirmed. "His uncle had a penchant for cages and used to keep a different girl there night after night." Cole shook his head. "You might not appreciate what you have, but I would ask you to be grateful. It seems Mr. Hyland really likes you." His focus fell to my exposed breasts. "And it's not very hard to see why."

"Oh God."

Closing my eyes, I tried to process what Cole told me. Saul and the others had mentioned Zander Hyland liked to cage and humiliate women he held captive, and it seemed as though some of his tastes had passed to his nephew, Sean.

"Come on." The pressure on my arm drew my attention back to the awful present. "He'll be waiting, and if I might offer some advice, you don't want to upset him at this juncture."

He was right, damn him. I knew he was, but my feet remained rooted to the spot.

"Miss Mantle?" Cole sounded impatient. "Please, let me escort you. If I have to ask one of Mr. Hyland's security men, your arrival will be a lot less dignified."

Glancing down at my exposed body, I could scarcely take another breath. How much less dignified could things get? I already knew the answer. One of those burly guys would pick me up, fling me over his shoulder, and carry me down the aisle like a sack of potatoes, with everything on show. Things were bad, but I wanted to cling to whatever modicum of self-respect I still had.

"Okay." With a sigh, I stepped forward, guided by Cole. "I don't want to do this, but okay." The knot of anxiety twisted at my pitiful admission. I was giving in again, allowing Hyland to infringe my rights, even though this was my best shot at liberty. Glancing behind me, I surveyed the route to freedom with desperate eyes.

"Please don't, Miss," Cole said as if he'd read my mind. "Mr. Hyland's men would find you, and he would make you pay."

Sniffing back tears, I realized he was correct again. I should just cede and accept my fate, but walking toward a life of servitude as Sean's unlucky wife was doing nothing to appease my worries.

"There you are." I glanced up to find one of Sean's colossal security guys looming by the entrance. "The boss is waiting. Let's move, darling," he smirked, his ugly mouth twisting into a grin as Cole supported me while I hobbled up the steps.

"The lady is negotiating her way in very perilous footwear." It was Cole who spoke on my behalf. "You can advise Mr. Hyland, she's on her way."

"Looks like you're enjoying your job a little too much there, old man." The hideous guy waiting at the door sneered as I finally made it to where he waited.

"Don't be crude," Cole retorted. "I am doing as Mr. Hyland ordered, not ogling his wife-to-be. Can you say the same?"

"If the boss hadn't wanted me to stare, why dress her like a whore?" The ugly stranger licked his lips, and instinctively, I recoiled, trying to pull away from Cole's grasp.

"What Mr. Hyland chooses is up to him." Cole was firm, just like his hold on me. "Now, I suggest you move out of our way and let the lady past."

"Don't see no lady here," the brawny idiot sniggered as he stepped aside. "But sure, Cole. Off you go."

With a sigh, Cole guided me into the vestibule, and just like my freedom, my days as a single woman seemed irrefutably doomed.

CHAPTER 18: SEAN

There she was—the woman I was going to marry. If you'd asked me, even a few short weeks ago, if I even wanted to wed, I'd have laughed in your face. Marriage was literally the last thing on my mind as I touched the ground in this shitty city, but it only went to illustrate what Zander always told me—you just never knew. Never knew which way the wind would blow, couldn't anticipate what your rivals would do, and never knew what life would throw at you. Watching as Cole left Hilary's side and, she inched up the long aisle in my direction, her chest heaving, I acknowledged just how right my uncle had been. Life had offered me Hilary, and rather than dismissing her, I'd opened my arms. In the limited time we'd been together, she had been the answer to many of the riddles I was here to solve. She focused my mind, helping to consolidate what Zander had left, and presenting the perfect opportunity to exact revenge on the son-of-a-bitch who'd slain my uncle in cold blood. In the meantime, she'd gifted me the perfect distraction, the best way to pass my time while I waited to clear up the mess Zander had left behind.

"She's lovely." Father Joseph leaned toward me, whispering over his prayer book. "Very appealing."

Grinning at his assessment, I straightened my lapels. "Just wait until you see her on her knees, Father."

Chuckling, he drew away, smoothing his vestments as we waited for Hilary's arrival. Father Jo had known me since I was a child, had overseen my confirmation, and listened to more than one of my confessions. He was the obvious choice to orchestrate my nuptials. Glancing over my shoulder, I acknowledged it was time. Swallowing the scrutiny of those I'd invited to bear witness to our union, my bride had finally tottered her way to the alter. I smiled as she took her place by my side.

"Beautiful."

It was only one murmured word, but it seemed to settle her. Maybe she was just pleased to have made it without incident, glad to have her back to the dozens of eyes now boring into her, though glancing down, her skirt was leaving little to their imaginations.

"Dearly beloved."

Father Joseph began, and my attention slid back to him, though all I could think about was Hilary—the fact I couldn't wait to get my hands on her, the fact she wasn't wearing anything under that skimpy dress, and the fact that very soon, she'd be all mine. Time moved in odd pockets throughout the ceremony, parts speeding up in my mind while others lingered, but it wasn't until the vows that my arousal truly soared. I'd asked Father Jo to shorten much of the ceremony, but this part was critical. I needed Hilary to be my good girl and play her part.

"And now for you, dear." He turned to her. "Repeat after me. I, Hilary Joanne Mantle, take thee, Sean Phillip Hyland, to be my wedded husband."

Hilary's gaze darted to me, her eyes screaming the unvocalized question—*how on earth had I known her full name when she'd never disclosed it?* Though, of course, of all her concerns, I was sure that was the least.

"Hilary?" The priest prompted her into life, and she parroted back the correct words. A pang of pride burgeoned at her compliance, especially when coupled with her fabulous tits. Maybe today really could be the best day of my life. I'd always assumed those sorts of quips were only for show.

"To have and to hold from this day forward, for better for worse, for richer for poorer, in sickness and in health…"

On the vows went, Hilary repeating the words like the compliant kitten I wanted, but next was the important line—the one where she'd need to admit obedience in front of God.

"To love, cherish, and to obey, 'til death do us part, according to God's holy ordinance, and thereto, I give thee my troth."

Father Joseph paused, looking at my bride for her lines, and it seemed every guest in the place paused, taking a breath. Face blushing, she swallowed, her gaze eventually landing on mine. This was it, the significance of this moment undeniable, and she sensed it as well.

"To love, cherish, and to…" Hesitating, she drew in a deep breath, suddenly unable to meet my eyes.

Obey. I sent the word to her with my powerful stare, knowing she could feel its weight, even if she refused to acknowledge it. *The word you're looking for is obey.*

"And to obey." Succumbing to the growing pressure, she mumbled the words but loud enough for the congregation to hear, a loud cheer rising from the pews at her admission. Hilary's cheeks burned even brighter as she was forced to wait until their applauds had died down before she could continue. I grinned as she forced out the final line, her gaze falling past her breasts to the floor.

"Very nice." I reached for her hand, squeezing it in a show of support. "And now, since you have made your vows in front of God, I ask Father Joseph if I can interrupt and take control of your wonderful mouth."

The priest smiled, already knowing what I had in mind. "Please do, my son."

Reaching into my inside pocket, my fingers found the special gag I'd purchased for the occasion. The ball was small, the plastic and strap white to match her attire, but nothing compared to her terrified expression when I pulled the thing free and turned, dangling it in front of those assembled.

"Now that she has agreed to obey, let us begin as we mean to continue!" Once more, a swell of praise rose from the men I'd invited. Turning, my brow arched at my bride. "Don't cause a fuss now," I warned, moving toward her. "Open up like a good girl."

"Sean." She mouthed my name, her breathy tone making me even harder than her wrenching humiliation.

"Open."

Outnumbered and hideously outmaneuvered, she accepted her plight, but there were tears in her eyes as her lips parted. Unmoved by her show of emotion, I shoved the white ball between her teeth and secured the strap behind her wonderful hair. Hilary had said everything she needed to say. I'd let her know when her mouth was required again.

Hilary

Shellshock. It was once how observers had described the effects of war—the stunned silence and ringing in the ears of victims, the aftermath of intense trauma. That was how it was for me, standing there, arms still bound, half of my body on display, and a new gag strapped in place. Now that I'd forced the vows out, my speaking was over. I'd fallen into the pits of matrimony with Sean, and my escape routes were closing one by one. Pulling in hot ribbons of air, I struggled for composure, to hear past the banging of my incessant heartbeat, to focus on the man in the robes officiating over this excuse of a ceremony, but no matter how hard I tried, that feat was impossible. Lips moved, twisting into suspicious smiles, and if I risked a glance over my shoulder, there were pews of people I didn't know, leering faces I didn't recognize, eyes drilling into me as they took in the skirt rising up my thighs and my shocked gagged expression. *This* —this was my nightmare playing out right in front of my eyes.

"Do you have the rings?"

The question floated past me, and turning back to Sean, another man I didn't know passed a velvet cushion in his direction. Scanning the surface, my gaze drank in the rings, rising back to the man about to become my husband.

"God will forgive if we improvise this section." The priest laughed. "It seems your bride is a little tied up."

Sean chuckled at the apparent quip. "That's true, Father. With this ring," he collected the larger of the two, sliding it onto his ring finger. "I thee wed."

Turning to me, his eyes shone, and the first time since I teetered to the altar, it was more than just satisfied glee I saw there. Collecting the smaller band, he walked around me, his breath hot at my neck.

"And I give you this ring as a token of my love and commitment, Hilary."

I twisted in time to see him crouch behind me, identifying the correct finger and slipping the jewelry into place. As he rose, our gazes locked.

"It's real platinum, of course. None of this gold crap." Sean resumed his place at my side, the priest grinning as he lifted his arms.

"Sean and Hilary, through their words today, have been joined together in holy wedlock."

My gaze fell to the priest's robes, though I could feel the intensity of Sean's stare.

"They have exchanged their vows before God and these witnesses, have pledged their commitment each to the other, and have declared the same by exchanging rings." The man in the vestments paused. "Well, almost exchanged them."

A rumble of laughter traveled around the vast space behind me.

"I now pronounce they are husband and wife." The priest glanced at Sean. "At this point, I would usually suggest you kiss the bride, my friend, but alas, it seems you have already found another use for her sweet lips."

"That's true, Father." Sean sniggered. "But worry not, I already have a substitute in mind, but it's not for the altar of my Lord."

My muscles tensed at the edgy quality of his voice.

"Of that, I have little doubt, my son." The priest's gaze flitted between Sean and me. "Then, you may lead your wife from God's altar and begin your new life together."

"Thank you, Father." There was a dark twinkle in Sean's gaze as he approached me. "I will." Clasping the leash still hanging between my exposed breasts, he glowered at me. "I'm going to free your hands now."

Tipping my head back to meet his fierce stare, I nodded, breathing in his spicy scent as he reached around me, tugging at the ribbon holding my wrists together.

"There." He grinned, wrapping the length of ribbon around my neck while I flexed my hands at my side. "Down now, wife. You're leaving this church as I expect you to be at all times unless otherwise commanded—on your hands and knees."

For one long moment, I thought my heart had stopped hammering altogether, his words echoing around my head long after his lips had stopped speaking. What? He expected me to crawl out of here? Yet even as I queried the logic, I caught sight of the way he twirled the end of the leash in his hand, and suddenly, it was obvious. Of course, he wanted me to crawl. This was Sean. He always wanted me to crawl.

"Now."

My knees buckled at the severity of his tone. I wanted to rip the plastic from my mouth and beg him to see reason, wanted to flee from the place with whatever decorum remained, but in the split second of intensity, all I could do was fold. As I crumpled to the carpeted altar, I despised myself for my weakness, loathed myself far more than I'd ever hated him. He was only a man—a man used to getting what he wanted—but I was used to men like that and experienced at deflecting their shit.

I should have known better.

CHAPTER 19: SAUL MORRISON

Tension gripped my stomach, reigniting the hurt that never went away, the gnawing strain that taunted me. Hilary was missing, but worse than that, she wasn't really missing at all. I knew exactly where she was, who had taken her—Sean fucking Hyland. My jaw tightened as his smug, ugly face burst into my mind. Sean had taken her, held her, and done God knew what, and in some lunacy, presumably designed to rile me, he intended to marry her. Today was that day. The day he planned to put a ring on her finger, and despite my every instinct to ride in there and save her, I was impotent.

"Fuck." The mounting pressure escaped in a low growl, my fingers grasping the tumbler of liquor even harder.

"Saul?" Dalton Reilly leaned toward me from the other side of the desk. "Are you okay?"

"Fine," I hissed, my eyes squeezing closed as I swallowed the lie. I'd never been farther from fine, a fact Dalton, one of my oldest friends, was well aware. Everything had disintegrated since Hilary slipped away, profits from The Syndicate, the organization I ran with his and his brother's help, had slumped, and the things I used to care about had suddenly lost their gloss.

"You'll get her back." Dalton's tone begged protest as if even he didn't believe the sentiment. "You know you will."

"Too late," I breathed out, though the apprehension furling inside knotted tighter. "It's too late. They're probably already married by now."

Checking my expensive wristwatch, I saw the clock ticking past three o'clock. Most church weddings happened by this time of day, and we knew from our investigation, the bastard was planning on getting hitched at St. Felix.

"I still don't understand why you don't just go down there and take her back."

I straightened at Connor Reilly's analysis. Dalton's younger brother had less finesse and far less concern about what people thought about him.

"Not helpful, Connor." Dalton snarled from beside him. "We've been through this already. We just took Zander Hyland out in a massive gunfight, and it's taken weeks of charm and money to iron out the creases that caused. We can't just blast our way into a fucking church and burn down another part of the capital." He threw Connor a knowing glower, the message in his gaze clear. *Don't start this shit again.*

"I'm just saying it's what I would have done." Connor shrugged, his dark hair falling into his green eyes. "But I get it. It's not so easy now."

"He's right." The words nearly stuck in my throat. "I should have just gone after her."

"No." Dalton's voice was emphatic. "You did the right thing, Saul."

"Right for who?" I snapped, anger pulsing from the clustering anxiety. "I noticed when it was your woman who was held by a Hyland, we went in all guns blazing, but we can't do the same for Hilary." Catching my breath, I fought to hold it together. "And she's one of us, too. Hilary worked for me for years."

"And been polishing your cock for the last few months." Connor's tone was wry.

"That's beside the point," I retorted, but it was precisely the point.

Hilary and I had been on the brink of a burgeoning relationship. The sex had been magnificent, and I really liked her. That was what really hurt—Hyland hadn't just taken a member of my payroll or my latest squeeze. He'd taken both, which was the point. He wanted to hit me where it smarted the most. He wanted to make me suffer, and grimly, I acknowledged it was working. I'd rarely felt as low as I had the last few days.

"You'll still get her back," Dalton assured me in his well-practiced tone. "We just have to be smarter than Sean Hyland. We need to find another way of bringing him down. One that doesn't involve a shootout in another London suburb."

Silence swirled around my office as his verdict hung in the air between us. Deep down, I knew he was right, and the logical part of my brain—the facet that had managed The Syndicate for decades—agreed, but my instincts were with Connor. They wanted to race over to the church and prise her from Hyland's twisted grasp. I dreaded to think what he'd done to her, but if I knew anything about that family, I was sure it was nothing good. Hyland men weren't capable of anything but greed and self-service. For the thousandth time today, panic clawed at my insides.

Hilary. My head fell, her name resonating around my head. *I'm so sorry, Hilary. You're not forgotten. Wherever you are, whatever he's doing to you, I'm going to get you back and make him pay.*

"Do we know where he's planning to take her after this façade?" I heard the strain in my voice, the way it trembled as I fought to contain my rising emotion.

"He's booked a couple of nights at The Ritz."

Lifting my chin at Connor's response, my jaw clenched. *The Ritz?* That was so fucking Hyland. They were all show and no substance. "And then?"

"We're working on it," Dalton assured me. "I agree with where your thoughts are going. Taking her from his private address will be far less traumatic than busting in during a church service."

"I never said that," I snapped at Dalton, yet again. Registering the flicker of hurt in his eyes, I turned away. I didn't know why I was being so hard on him. The Syndicate had acted to protect its members with dull regularity. It wasn't as if his woman, Delilah, was the first we'd rushed in to protect, but I couldn't stop drawing the comparison, couldn't vanquish the nagging feeling Delilah had been worth putting our necks on the line for, but Hilary wasn't. This wasn't Dalton's fault—I knew it wasn't—but I couldn't suppress the resentment bubbling below the surface. "I just want to be armed with all the facts."

"Okay." He raised his palms in a conciliatory manner. "I'll double down our efforts and get you an address by the end of today."

He sensed it, too. I knew him well enough to recognize that. Even though Dalton wasn't culpable, he felt guilty about the way things had played out.

"Thanks."

Blowing out another breath, my gaze flitted from him back to Connor, agitation swelling. Why were we just sitting here talking? Anything could be happening while we ruminated on the problem. Sean might have married her by now, might have taken her back to The Ritz and screwed her. My toes curled inside the Italian leather on my feet, the mental image torturing me. If he hurt one fucking hair on her head, I would slice the vermin up so small, the worms wouldn't even have to chew. I would destroy him.

"Anything else?" Dalton sounded hopeful, the tone grating. How dare he be so optimistic? How dare he pretend things were okay? No doubt he had plans for the afternoon, and Delilah was waiting on his return...

"Why?" I couldn't contain the sarcastic streak his query stirred. "Do you have somewhere else to be?"

"Saul." Once more, a pained expression lit his face. "I didn't mean it like that, and you know it."

"Okay, I'm sorry." It wasn't like me to be so petulant, and Hilary wasn't exactly the first woman I'd lost. I had to get a grip on these feelings, had to *do something*... "Go if you need to, Dalton. Just let me know when you figure out where that son-of-a-bitch is taking her."

"I will." He rose, straightening his suit. "We'll figure this out, Saul." He flashed those big blue eyes at me. "You know it upsets me to see you this way."

"I know." I wanted to go to him, to embrace him and tell him everything was cool. Dalton was like a brother to me, they both were, but I couldn't make my feet move, couldn't get the words out. I wanted to forgive him, work through these toxic emotions, and in time, I would, but right now, things were too raw. "Thanks."

Turning to his brother, he shoved his fists into his jacket pockets. "Connor, are you coming?"

"In a minute." Connor flashed him a smile. "I'll meet you at Diablo."

"Okay." Dalton's gaze slid from Connor to me, and it was obvious he had an opinion about leaving the two of us to talk, though wisely, he kept it to himself. "See you both soon."

I watched as he closed the door behind him, silence filling the air as Connor waited in front of me.

"Something you want to say?" I asked, arching a brow at the younger man.

I'd always liked both Reilly men, but over the years, Connor had been more like a son to me, especially in the wake of his own parents' death. He was as suave and good-looking as his brother, but there was always something edgier, something reckless. I'd had to pick him up from numerous falls since he'd gone his own way, patch up many mistakes, from breaking him out of jail to covering up murder. Connor was dangerous, and sometimes, that wild streak was useful. Sometimes, it was just what life needed.

"Yes." He leaned closer, his arms pressed on the huge desk. "I want to help you, Saul, wanna be useful in a way I know Dalton can't."

"Can't or won't?" My tone was sardonic.

"I'm not here to discuss Dalton." His retort shut down my cynicism, reminding me of the man who sat in front of me—a man who took chances, a man anyone considering a fool-hardy plan would want by their side.

"Okay." I leaned back in my chair. "Go on."

"I know what's on your mind." His green eyes burned into me. "I know that look on your face. I've seen it before."

"Oh, yeah?" I sighed, swirling the whiskey in my glass. It was really too early to be indulging in hard liquor, but these days, I didn't give a shit. "Where have you seen it?"

"In the mirror." Connor's tone was hard and even.

"What do you mean?"

"I mean, I know what's on your mind." Connor's stare

drilled into me. "What keeps you awake at night, and I know what you want to do once you leave this room."

"I don't know what you're talking about." Something about his intensity was making me uncomfortable, and reflexively, I shifted in my seat.

"Don't give me that bullshit. It's written all over your face, Saul. I could read it when you spoke to Dalton."

Christ, was I truly so easy to decipher? Lifting the glass to my lips, my brow furrowed as I regarded Connor.

"All I'm saying is… I understand." Passion seared his tone as he went on. "I know where you're coming from, and I'm prepared to help."

The alcohol burned as it passed down my throat.

"I also understand Dalton isn't." He drew in a deep breath. "But that's okay, too. I know some guys who are prepared to support what we're going to do."

"What *we're* going to do?" I repeated slowly, trying to make sense of it.

"That's right." An errant smile stretched across Connor's face. "Dalton might be afraid of a little peril, but I'm not, and I know exactly how we can do it."

"How we can do what?" I pushed him for clarification, the tension rising in me in waves.

"What?" Connor laughed, shaking his head as if I was an idiot. "Well, that's the easy part, Saul. How we're going to get your woman back. Today."

CHAPTER 20: SEAN

This was my moment. For years, I'd played in the sun, dallying in work, women, and fine wine, while committing to none of them. It had taken Zander's slaying and coming back to this gray cesspit for me to finally find my place—to find Hilary, the woman now kneeling by my side. Casting an eye over her, pride ballooned in my chest. She was my wife, which meant she'd always be more than those cheap floozies.

Tugging the leash, I reminded her why she was on her hands and knees—to follow—and pacing away, I urged her forward. This was the metaphor for our marriage. I would lead, and she would follow, though whether it would ever be as spectacular as this again remained to be seen.

Glancing down at her, crawling by my feet, I beamed. Hilary was so fucking delectable with her mouth gagged with the fetching white ball and her wonderful assets hanging in front of her. Dropping back, I took a moment to appreciate the rear view as well, her wiggling hips presenting her shaven pussy to me and the rest of the congregation. Worship had never looked so good.

"Congratulations, Sean!" Arthur Noble, one of Zander's old allies, stepped out of a nearby pew, stretching his hand toward me.

Like most of the guests, he had been invited for his status and influence. Every man in the church was responsible for some aspect of the Hyland brand, and I'd gathered them here today to send a message—Zander might be dead, but the Hyland empire was not. I was back. I ran the show.

"Gotta say, I never thought I'd see the day you settled down, but believe me, I understand the appeal." His gaze fell to Hilary, hungry eyes assessing her firm breasts until a spike of envy rose in me.

"Yeah, well, you know what they say, Arthur?" I reached for his palm with my free hand, shaking it firmly. "Once you meet the right woman, it's over."

He grinned. "Yes indeed."

"You're welcome to stay and celebrate with us." Looking up, I caught the eyes of the many well-wishers who'd convened to ogle my bride. "That counts for you all. The Ritz has a suite waiting for us."

"Too kind." Joud Cohen stepped forward from the throng, lips curling. "But then, if there's one thing you Hylands are good at, it's revelry." His smile broadened, revealing a line of crooked teeth.

"That and business, eh?" I met his outstretched hand.

"Right," Joud agreed. "Speaking of which, will you be honoring your late uncle's contracts?"

"Now is not the time, my friend." I gestured to my wife on her hands and knees. "I just married the woman of my dreams. We're here to honor that union, not contracts."

"Forgive me." Lifting his palms in the air, Joud nodded. "I totally understand. We shall talk business another day."

With a nod, I waited for the throng to part, creating a

walkway for us, and head held high, I led Hilary out of the church.

Hilary

My head throbbed with the ignominy, the knowledge that every pair of eyes in the place was trained on us, and no doubt, enjoying the sight of my utter debasement, reinforced by the reality, there was little I could do to prevent my misery. Pressing my palms into the hard church floor, my head fell forward with the weight of my shame. I supposed I could have jumped to my feet and gotten into a brawl with Sean to wrangle the leash from his grasp or unclip the thing from my neck, but the idea of drawing yet more attention to myself was paralyzing. *Better just get this over and done with. Crawl as fast as you can and get the fuck out of here.* Of course, I should have known better. Sean insisted on pausing to make small talk with those assembled, and inevitability, they all seemed to be vile, leering men. Pulling in a heaving breath, I denied the tears burning in my eyes, just as I ignored the saliva gathering at the corners of the gag.

This wasn't happening. It couldn't be happening.

After what seemed like an age, the entrance to the church loomed, and while the prospect of crawling across gravel offered little in the way of a reprieve, it did at least signify the end of this latest ordeal.

"On your knees."

My muscles tensed at Sean's command, and gingerly, I lifted my head as I rose to a kneeling position.

"You've done well."

I couldn't even turn his way to acknowledge the alleged praise, my gaze taking in the waiting limo and the light outside.

"Time to carry you the rest of the way."

He moved like lightning, reaching for me in a heartbeat and lifting me from the ground into his arms. Much though I didn't want to welcome the embrace of the man who'd put me through this torment, I flung my arms around him. I loved him. I hated him. Despised what he'd helped me become but wanted him more than ever. None of it made any bloody sense—it never had.

"Come on."

Burying my face in his shoulder, I was aware of the change in temperature as he negotiated the steps and carried me to the car.

"Congratulations, Mr. and Mrs. Hyland."

I recognized Cole's voice but still couldn't bring myself to react to it. He represented the outside world, a place I had no desire to live in until the fragments of this searing shame slipped away.

"Thank you, Cole." Sean, on the other hand, sounded genuinely happy. "Take us to The Ritz."

Lowering me into the car, I was conscious of the way he slid onto the leather, pulling me closer to his body when the door slammed shut.

"We did it," he whispered into my hair, stroking the side of my face as he arranged me on his lap. "Congratulations, Hilary Hyland."

Hilary Hyland. I shivered, shifting to straddle him. Was that my name now? Had I agreed to that?

His hand moved to my face, catching the falling tears, then lowered to tug the gag from my lips.

"No more tears now." The order was gentle but firm. "Today's a happy day."

I met his gaze, my head still heavy. "I don't know what to say, Sir."

What the hell did he want me to say? Against my every instinct, he'd persuaded me to go through with this madness, and now it was done. I was his fucking wife.

"Say you're looking forward to tonight." His gaze widened as numerous salacious thoughts likely swirled in his head. "To me putting you out of your misery."

No matter how much I wanted to protest the point, he was right. I yearned for him to extinguish the blaze burning inside me, flames he had lit and stoked every day of my incarceration. He was the door I just couldn't close, the yearning with no apparent end.

"Oh God." I crumpled, despite his instruction, only vaguely aware of the vehicle moving as I pressed my face into his suit jacket.

"Hilary." He laughed gently, burying his fingers in my hair and tugging my face away from his shoulder. "It's okay. It's done."

Gasping for air, I met his gaze with teary eyes.

"You really mean it, Sir?" I wanted to believe him, to have faith in his word, but after everything, I was having a problem trusting anything he said.

"Yes, I mean it," he assured me. "Later, after we've celebrated, I'm going to detonate you, beautiful. Send you higher than you've ever known."

That sounded so good. I needed it so much, and I deserved it. I'd put up with all his bullshit, been denied and tormented for so long.

"And afterward?"

"Afterward, we honeymoon." His voice was like honey,

smooth and sweet as it floated past my ears. "You get to finesse your submission, and I get to indulge my new wife."

"That sounds nice." I hated myself for admitting it, but fuck, if I had to spend the rest of my life agonizing over not only the demands Sean made but the way I reacted to them, let there be some indulgence as well. It may be selfish, but I didn't care.

"It will be." Grabbing my arse with one hand, he twirled my hair with the fingers of the other, cradling the back of my head. "I have so much to offer you, Hilary Hyland."

My breath caught at the sound of my new name, the resonance not nearly as bad as I recalled.

"I know I expect a lot, and I'm not apologizing for anything, but if you only worship me, I can give you the world in return."

He made it all sound so simple as if I was giving up a week in the Canary Islands, but as ever, whether it was the humiliation, dehydration, or the constant thrum of my arousal, I melted, succumbing to his will. That's how it had been right from the start. I'd fucking loathed him, but Sean had a way of melding with me, smiling until I surrendered, then laughing as the first wave of defeat consumed me.

"I've got the empire, baby." He smiled, displaying pretty white teeth that would have made any dentist proud. "You've got the heart. Just imagine what we can create together."

"Speaking of which, Sir." I swallowed, suddenly recalling the concern which had flitted into my mind during the brief moments of lucidity.

"Yes?" His brow rose at my change of tack.

"When we fuck, I'll need some sort of contraception." It should have been hideous to discuss such personal matters with him, but after everything he'd put me through, the embarrassment barely registered, and anyway, my choice or not, he was my husband now.

"Is that what you're worried about?" His hand relaxed, ruffling my hair as if I was the cutest, most naïve thing he'd ever laid eyes on.

"Yes, but..." My brow creased. Couldn't he see this was important? The last thing I needed was a fucking pregnancy to manage in this shit show. "It's pretty significant, Sir."

"It's taken care of, gorgeous." Reaching forward, he pressed a chaste kiss to my forehead.

"What?" Leaning back, I caught his eyes. "What do you mean?"

"I mean, it's been dealt with." He smiled. "I guess you don't remember?"

"No." I shook my head. "When was it dealt with?"

"During the first few days after the basement, I had Johnson give you the contraceptive shot." His smile widened. "He gave me the rundown on its efficacy, and based on the fact you haven't bled since I've had you, you should be protected by now."

"W-Wait, who is Johnson?" My head was about to burst with confusion.

Sean arched an eyebrow at me, and God help me, I reacted just the way he wanted, stuttering as I tried to respond as soon as I could.

"S-Sir."

"He's my doctor." Once again, he smirked, his expression sympathetic. "He's the one who sedated you that first time on the street."

I could vaguely recall the man he spoke about, an involuntary shudder passing through me at the memory. "He gave me another injection?" It was starting to make sense, but still, I couldn't believe it, couldn't fathom how these men—men like Sean—could consistently violate my rights and take control of my body.

"That's right," he soothed. "It should last a while, so no need to worry about little Hylands for a while."

My throat dried at his casual quip. Of course, I was glad to hear there wouldn't be any unplanned pregnancies, but the news was a shock, nonetheless. "I don't know what to say, Sir."

"A thank you will suffice." He chuckled, drawing my face closer to his. "Nothing is going to get in the way of our first night as man and wife, Hilary."

I stared into his eyes, and despite the disbelief radiating through me, his hungry gaze stirred something, stoking the fire he'd already built. If this was to be my fate, then let him be right. Tonight, we would set the fucking world on fire.

CHAPTER 21: SEAN

Shrugging my Versace jacket from my shoulders, I wrapped it around her, helping her slip her tiny arms inside. For once, I was feeling generous, aware we were about to step foot inside one of the most glamorous hotels on the planet, and I was conscious of her modesty. That was laughable after I'd paraded her around St. Felix's like my personal pet, but it mattered to her. Her expression relaxed as she snuggled inside its warmth.

"Thank you, Sir." Gratitude flashed in her eyes as Cole parked the car outside the entrance. "I appreciate it."

"Do up the front," I reminded her just as Cole opened the door. "We don't want every passerby on Piccadilly getting an eyeful, do we?"

"No, Sir." She blushed, the sweetest look lighting her face —part disbelief I should care and part agreement.

"Out you get." I nodded to the open door, noticing the smile Cole offered as he guided her to the path. I joined her a moment later, dispatching my driver with a simple nod.

"Come on, Mrs. Hyland." Slipping a possessive arm around her middle, I grasped her tighter to me as we cut a path to the double doors. The uniformed doorman acknowledged us as we slipped inside to the front desk.

The Ritz was every inch what I recalled. Enveloped with style and historic elegance, it had something to cater to every appetite, as long as you had the budget to afford it. Fortunately, thanks to Zander, money was no object. Glancing at Hilary, I realized I wanted to spend it on her. I might have gone to the trouble of ensuring my assets were protected if she ever tried to leave me, but that didn't change my desire to spoil her and spend every day showing her what her submission would merit.

"Mr. and Mrs. Hyland." The man behind the desk flashed me a well-practiced smile. "Congratulations. We've been expecting you."

Of course, they had. My people had contacted them days ago to ensure the wedding breakfast met my requirements, and naturally, I'd secured The Prince of Wales suite for the next few days. If we were stuck in this dreary city, we might as well make the best of it.

"Thank you." I met his smile with one of my own, relishing the way my new wife not only held her tongue without the use of the gag, now safely tucked away in the pocket of the jacket swamping her flawless body, but how she leaned into me, apparently seeking the comfort of my body. That was encouraging. Perhaps there was hope for our union, after all? I'd known our sexual chemistry could set the hotel ablaze but hadn't expected such tenderness. "I believe we have a suite waiting for us."

"Yes, sir." Glancing down at his screen, he nodded. "William Kent House has been prepared for you and your guests. One of my colleagues can take you there, and I believe your luggage has already been sent to your personal suite?"

"That's right," I concurred, my lips twitching at Hilary's wide-eyed reaction. "My driver brought it over earlier this morning."

"Very good, sir." The man's eyes sparkled. "Everything is in place."

"Thank you." Lowering my face to nuzzle her honeyed tresses, my gaze darted back to the face of the knowing receptionist. "We'll go through now."

"Very good, sir."

I waited while he signaled to a colleague, excited about the day of indulgence that lay ahead. A younger guy wandered toward us, smiling.

"Please, follow me, sir."

"Come on, darling." I nudged Hilary, aware of the small smile on her lips. Her tears were finally dry, and if I wasn't mistaken, she was actually enjoying herself, although how long that would last once she realized what I had in mind remained to be seen.

It was a short walk to William Kent House, passing through the luxurious interior of the hotel into the equally breathtaking surroundings of our wedding reception.

"Here we are." The younger man beamed, pausing in The Great Hall. "The William Kent Room is prepared for your wedding breakfast, but please, feel free to make use of any of the rooms here, and don't hesitate to let us know if you require anything further."

Thanking him, I dismissed the nearby staff members before I took her hand and led her through The Queen Elizabeth Room to the place prepared for us to eat.

"Sean." Awe resonated from her voice. "Sir, this is amazing!"

Lifting my chin, I gazed around at the exquisite furnishings. Stylish architecture met the finest décor, just as it did everywhere at The Ritz.

"I'm pleased you like it," I murmured, squeezing her hand.

"It must have cost the earth." Shaking her head, she gazed to the high ceiling before her attention flitted back to me. "I've never seen anything like it."

Resisting the urge to query why Morrison had never taken her here, I merely grinned and pulled her flush against me. My hands ran over her skirt, skimming beneath it to grab her delectable backside. Running my fingers between her cheeks, they grazed the butt plug still lodged deep inside her, and right on cue, my cock swelled. I would be there soon, along with every other place I wanted to explore.

"Don't worry about the money. We can afford it."

"I didn't think you wanted me to spend your money." She fluttered her lashes at me, gazing up into my eyes. "Wasn't that what the trip to Mr. Crane's office was about?"

I was surprised she wanted to recollect much of that day, but running my tongue over my teeth, I was happy to dwell on all its wonderful depravity.

"That was only about what happened in the event of our separation." I breathed in the scent of her again. "Which is not going to happen."

"So, you don't mind if I spend it?" Her brow rose as she lifted to her tiptoes and brushed her lips over my chin. "Sir?"

"No," I assured her. "It's yours to spend, gorgeous, when I give you enough time to do so."

"Really?" She sucked her lower lip between her teeth. "Planning on keeping me busy, Sir?"

I wasn't sure who the temptress cavorting in my arms was, but I had to admit, I liked her.

"Oh, yes," I growled. "You'll be tied up with your responsibilities most of the time."

"Responsibilities, Sir?"

Fuck, she was so enticing, I could have eaten her up on the spot.

"To my cock." Arching a brow, I relished the deep rush of color that flooded her cheeks, along with her mischievous smile. "Don't forget all the lessons I've taught you."

"How could I when you're such a patient tutor?" Her voice was breathless.

"I'll be with you every step of the way, baby." Fisting her hair, I drew her face to me. "And once I make you mine, our life together truly begins."

A cough in the doorway pulled my focus from Hilary to one of the staff.

"My apologies, sir," he started, shifting his weight.

"What is it?" I snapped. Hadn't I already told them we didn't want to be disturbed?

"Your guests have started to arrive, sir." He blanched at my response. "They're waiting in the Grand Hall."

"Ensure their glasses are filled." I relaxed. "Mrs. Hyland and I are just going to explore The William Kent Room."

"Very good, sir."

"Come on." I tugged her arm from around me and guided her into the next room. "I think you'll like this one."

She came to an abrupt halt in the doorway, her jaw dropping at the crimson expanse of the room. As requested, the long table was dressed to perfection, with golden candelabra lighting the walls as well as the dining area.

"Wow." Taking a step forward, her gaze drank in the lavish surroundings. "Sean." Turning, she spun to regard me. "This is insane. It's too much."

"Not for you," I assured her, closing the distance between us with an easy stride. "Not for us."

Closing her mouth, she gazed up at the chic furnishings, genuinely stunned into submission. That was a first.

"You like?" I goaded playfully.

"I more than like," she answered, reaching for my chin with her tiny hand. "Thank you, Sir."

"You're welcome," I purred. "As I remember, I still owe you a first kiss."

Her gaze lowered coyly. "Yes, Sir, I believe you do."

Capturing her face in my hands, I swooped.

Nothing I wanted would ever be denied me.

CHAPTER 22: HILARY

My head was spinning. One moment, Sean had been the usual arrogant arsehole, the man who'd leashed me and demanded I take our journey down the aisle as husband and wife on my hands and knees, but the next, he was quite different. This version of the man had offered me dignity with his jacket and seemed to delight in showing me the extraordinary setting his money had bought us. I had to admit, The Ritz was like nothing I'd known. It was a setting for dreams, an environment crafted for Kings and Ambassadors.

Back in the Grand Hall, I blinked at the enormous spiral staircase, wondering what my life had become. Finally, on my feet again, I was permitted my second glass of champagne and an introduction to some of the unknown guests Sean had invited. If I dwelled on the recent experience at the church and the fact they had no doubt seen me, I could have drowned in my mortified embarrassment, but Sean had a way of guiding me through the maze of strangers, drawing me into conversation and keeping me close. Maybe it was the alcohol, but for the first time, I actually felt like his partner rather than just the assistant of his greatest rival—the woman he'd captured.

Saul. My brow furrowed. Turning from the conversation with some businessman or another, Sean's hand still snaking around my hips, I imagined Saul. How long had it been since I'd seen him, since we'd talked and fucked? Anxiety curled in my belly at the unsettling thought, but it subsided with another—*where had Saul been all this time?* Where was he when I'd needed him, when I'd been kidnapped for Sean's amusement? After all the years I'd worked for him, I assumed he'd come for me, at least try to save me from this life, but now, it was too late. Sean had a ring on my finger. I lifted the digit in question, examining the band of metal he'd placed there.

"Looks as if your new wife likes her wedding ring."

The gray-haired man we'd been talking to laughed at my vacant expression, and squeezing me closer, Sean joined him.

"You can't blame her," he teased. "She's never been married before, but then, neither have I."

"That's true," the stranger concluded. "And let me say, you make an exceptionally handsome couple. I'm sure you'll enjoy a wonderful marriage, despite the unconventional beginnings."

I flushed at his astute analysis. Did everyone here know my story? That I'd been Sean's captive? Lifting my flute to my lips, I supposed they did. It seemed I was to have no secrets in this new world.

"Ladies and gentlemen!" The master of ceremonies called from the corner of Grand Hall, attracting the attention of everyone assembled. "We ask that you be seated in The William Kent Room."

I watched, smiling politely as the group of guests trailed out of the hall. The vast majority of them were men much older than Sean and me, but I noticed a few now had female partners in tow. I took a gulp of alcohol, glad they'd missed the shame of the service. Glancing down, I realized I was still draped in Sean's jacket, the only thing preserving what little remained of my modesty.

"Ready for your first meal as a married woman?"

I turned at his query, acknowledging it had sparked a flurry of nerves. Suddenly, this was real. The farce that had been the church service was easy to recall as a lurid nightmare, but the opulence of The Ritz meant this aspect of the day would forever be scorched into my mind.

"Yes, Sir."

Taking the arm he offered and still clutching my champagne flute, we walked the short distance to our wedding breakfast. A rapturous round of applause broke out as we entered the magnificent scarlet room, and for once, my blushes were welcome as I acknowledged the well wishes.

Sean led me to one of the two vacant chairs, whispering for me to sit. I obeyed quickly, pleased to shift some of the focus from me for a change. Placing my glass on the beautifully dressed table, I waited for my new husband to join me.

"I'd like to take this opportunity, on behalf of my beautiful bride and myself, to thank each and every one of you for joining us." Raising his flute, he offered the toast, accepting the applause. "If you attended our church service, you'll remember I forfeited the right to kiss my bride since her mouth was otherwise engaged."

A rumble of throaty laughter danced around the table. Lowering my gaze, I shifted awkwardly on my chair. Why was he bringing this up again?

"Now, we're all here reveling in the rich abundance of The Ritz," Sean continued, his gaze traveling along the line of those seated. "I'd like to enjoy the substitute instead."

I straightened, something in his words stirring the apprehension his kindness had only just put to bed.

"So, if you'd all raise your glasses, I'll propose a toast to the bride!"

"Sean," I hissed, willing him to just be quiet and sit down. Hadn't I been embarrassed enough today?

"To the bride!" The words rang out from all sides of the room, and uneasily, I smiled at the dozens of eyes boring into me.

"And now, my love." Sean put down his glass, his attention turning to me. "Rather than a first kiss, I'm giving a first spanking." Edging his seat back, he perched on the red velvet cushion, beckoning me with a finger.

"What?" I whispered, though the room was so silent now, no doubt everyone heard me.

"Our first spanking as a married couple." His brow arched. "Don't make me wait, baby."

"But..." My gaze darted around the table wildly. Surely, he couldn't be serious, couldn't expect to fling me over his lap here and now, in front of all our well-dressed guests and The Ritz staff? The knotting tension in my tummy and the brooding look in his eyes conveyed the truth—that was exactly what he expected.

"Now."

His tone lowered to the octave that caused my heart to race, and flustering, I rose from my chair, shuffling toward him. A part of me still couldn't fathom what was happening, couldn't conceive the fact he wanted to humiliate me here—of all places—but I knew any complaint would only exacerbate my plight.

"Leave my jacket on your chair."

My eyes widened as my gaze darted back to my seat. I wanted to insist I stay clothed, but I couldn't bring myself to plead in front of these strangers—men and women who'd never met me before but would likely never forget Sean's blushing bride. I fiddled with the buttons, my hands trembling as my pulse pounded, and as if someone had hit slow motion, I shrugged the warmth of his jacket from my skin, dropping it on the cushion behind me. From the other end of the table, a wolf whistle filled the air, followed by a fresh wave of laughter. Cringing, I moved toward him, almost grateful to be flung over his lap. It was absolutely dreadful to be exposed and shamed this way, but at least upturned, I couldn't bear witness to the ecstatic expressions of those assembled.

Sean wasted no time in warming me up, his palm hitching up my pathetically short skirt and crashing onto my bared bottom before I got my bearings. A wail of glee burst from the guests.

"This is for you, my love!" Sean sounded delirious, desperately happy at my chastened and dishonored position. "A reminder of your place and what awaits you in our marriage."

"Here, here!" A male voice echoed from ahead somewhere. "I am all in favor of this kind of marriage."

Another roll of amusement crashed around me, but I couldn't concentrate on that ignominy, Sean's hand peppering my backside and taking my breath away. Each swat was hard, the short, insistent slaps catching the vulnerable underside of my cheeks, the hurt vibrating to the plug wedged between them, ensuring it was impossible to keep still.

"Seems like she enjoys it!"

I squeezed my eyes closed, my jaw tightening at the next round of smacks, though the nagging paranoia remained. Was the casual observer correct—beneath this show of pain and protest, was my pussy secretly yearning for more of the treatment?

"You have no idea." Sean chuckled as he rained down the strikes, his palm alternating cheeks in a depraved show of authority. "There's no doubt I am one lucky son-of-a-bitch."

"I'll drink to that!"

Another voice echoed from the other side of the table, and gasping, I imagined them all peering over the fancy spread to witness my denigration. No doubt, some had risen from their seats and found new, better positions to view me. Maybe the staff had decided to relish the show, too.

"Oh God." The mewl slipped from me as my hands balled into fists. I didn't know what I'd expected from the day, but it hadn't been this! It hadn't been one round of public disgrace after the next. I prayed for the onslaught to stop, for his palm to pause and let me catch my breath, but the reprieve never came. Sean spanked me, matching the glib comments of his guests as his hand humbled and humiliated. By the time amnesty was finally offered, the tears had formed again, my face probably as red as my backside.

"There." Resting the palm which had taken such pleasure in my punishment, Sean patted my flesh in a cruelly tender way.

The tiny act of compassion riled me. How dare he do this? How dare he do any of this? One moment, he used and abused me, and the next, he sought to show sympathy—the man was absurd.

"That concludes the first spanking."

I panted as another low peal of laughter rumbled around the room.

"Ladies and gentlemen, please enjoy your meal."

CHAPTER 23: SAUL

"You're sure this can work?" Adrenaline raced through my body, excitement simmering for the first time in too long. "You're serious about this?"

"Deadly." Connor's lips curled. "Do I commit to things I'm not serious about?"

He had a point. Whenever Connor made his mind up about something, anything, few powers on earth could hold him back, least of all me. The last significant decision he'd made had been to induct his lover, Molly, into our organization—an audacious plan in its own right, but all the more spectacular after having kidnapped her and enticed her back from the United States. He had a rare ability to understand the possible ramifications of his choices and still choose carnage, but he was also a winner. Connor could take a blow and go the distance. All those years of martial arts competitions I'd taken him to as a teen had proved that.

"No." I nodded in acknowledgment. "No, you don't, but I just want to be sure how many men you have ready. We'll need a few to tear into the church and seize her."

"The Ritz," he corrected me calmly.

"What?" Sitting up in my chair, I slammed my glass on my desk.

"The. Ritz." He enunciated as if I hadn't heard him properly the first time, but I'd heard him just fine. The Ritz was one of the most prestigious hotels in the city. We couldn't just wander in there and spray the place with bullets.

"The service will be over by now."

A part of my heart crumpled, though deep down, I knew it to be true.

"Better we hit them at the next known location."

"The reception?" My head was swimming, not only from the alcohol fogging it. I couldn't envision the plan Connor suggested.

"The honeymoon suite." Connor shifted in his chair. "We know they're booked into The Prince of Wales suite, and let's face facts, it'll be a lot easier to bring Sean to heel once he's alone and has his mind on bedding his bride."

"Don't." My hands balled into fists at the idea of what he would do to Hilary there. "I just… can't think about that."

"So, don't think about it." Connor shrugged. "I'm still right."

There was the Reilly arrogance I'd known for so long. Connor was like Teflon—however dirty the aftermath, nothing ever stuck to him.

"You're right."

It scarcely pained me to admit it anymore. This was about Hilary, about saving her from Hyland's grimy grasp. I didn't understand what I felt for her, but whatever had happened between her and Sean, she was on my mind all the time. I needed closure almost as much as she needed rescue. I should have taken affirmative action days ago, and I would have if I had pinned down where he was hiding her. It had taken the wedding to bring them out of seclusion.

"I'm glad you think so." He leaned back in his chair self-righteously. "To answer your concern, I have eight other guys, ten of us in total."

"You're coming?"

Not that it mattered. *I* would take this chance, risk it all for Hilary, but I didn't want to assume his participation. It had taken an injection of his enthusiasm to see past Dalton's logic, to make this plan a reality, but now that I had it, I would take it on, alone if I had to.

"Of course, I am." Connor laughed. "This imbecile is clearly just like his uncle. He needs to be taken down a notch or twenty, and I'm just the man to help. It was always going to be me, Saul." His grin grew. "Dalton is too caught up in what happened with Delilah. The memories are too raw."

"Of course." For the first time in too long, a twinge of guilt bloomed. I had been nothing but a sod to Dalton, rude and irate since Hilary was snatched. In reality, all he'd done was support me, The Syndicate, and do everything he could to protect the woman he loved. I'd been a swine. "I've been a wanker to him."

"He'll get over it." Connor smiled. "Dalton's a big boy."

"Yeah." I sighed, reaching for my glass of water. It was time to sober up and start thinking straight. "I'll speak to him properly when all of this is over."

"He'll be thrilled when he finds out." Connor flashed those perfect teeth at me. "You know how much he loves a gunfight."

"He'll get over it." I intentionally copied Connor's earlier words. "It is still me who runs this show. He'll have to live with my choices."

"Great." Connor clapped his hands, his enthusiasm for the

brewing plan more than clear. "Midnight it is. We'll meet in the car park."

"Why so late?"

I didn't know why I was pushing the point. Connor had already explained the logic, but all I could think about were the things Hyland would be doing to Hilary in the interim. I gulped down the hideous thoughts, draining the rest of the water.

"By then, they're sure to be on their own." He went through the reasoning, though I could tell he was exasperated. "That's what we want. It gives us the maximum chance of success. We'll have the element of surprise, and his guard will be on the floor. How many men expect to be ambushed on their wedding night?" Connor's face lit up at the sound of his own plan.

"None," I concurred. His reasoning was sound, even if I wanted to vomit at the idea of waiting. Connor had a plan, which was more than I had half an hour ago. Even if they were married and had consummated that union, it didn't matter. I would still take her back and pay for the very best divorce lawyer money could buy. I'd unravel Hilary from that bastard if it was the last thing I did.

"Midnight, it is."

"Good." Connor stood, thrusting his palm in my direction. "Until then, don't let on to Dalton. The last thing we need is hours of him lecturing us about our scheme."

"Not a problem." I grasped his hand and shook it firmly. "He won't hear it from me."

"We'll take two of the black sedans," he went on matter-of-factly. "Cars that don't arouse suspicion and are instantly forgettable. We'll enter from both sides of Piccadilly and take the staff entrances at the back of the building."

"Okay." All of a sudden, Connor was in charge, making

the rules and giving the orders. It might have been disconcerting had I not needed his morale so badly. "And bring plenty of weaponry. An arsehole like Hyland will be armed, wedding night or not."

"Oh, I hope so." Connor chuckled, his hand falling to his side. "I'm counting on it."

CHAPTER 24: SEAN

So, this was wedded bliss. Stretching back in the large armchair provided by The Queen Elizabeth Room, I marveled at how long it had taken me to capture it, my attention sliding inevitably to the bride who had made the impossible a reality. Balancing on all fours, she was naked, the attempt at a gown I'd bought discarded after we'd eaten. She'd been gagged and shackled, though I'd gone to great lengths to ensure the chains running between her wrists and ankles were white and her wonderful firm breasts were decorated with the clamps I'd brought along for the occasion. Small and silver, each was adorned with a tiny bell, which chimed whenever she moved. I smiled at the sound as she shifted on her hands and knees, reaching down to stroke her backside. Still plugged and glowing from her recent spanking, her arse was on display for all our guests to see, but only I would get to enjoy it.

"Sean." Tony Peel loomed over me, grinning as he took in the plight of my new wife. "No, don't get up. I just wanted to thank you both for my invitation. Sindy and I have had a great time."

Gesturing toward the brown-eyed woman fidgeting beside him, my focus flitted to Sindy. She couldn't be more than twenty, while Zander's old friend, Tony, was fast approaching his dotage. "I like the way your marriage is working out. It's nice to see such a compliant wife."

"Thank you, and you're welcome." Extending my long legs, I rested my shoes on the small of Hilary's back, laughing darkly. "She also doubles as a fine footrest. Fancy it, Sindy?"

Her face erupted in a hot blush as she glanced down at Hilary. Right on cue, my bride swayed, the motion causing the minute bells to tinkle.

"Er, no, thank you." Sindy shifted awkwardly.

"Perhaps I need to upgrade!" Tony roared with laughter, beaming at his date's obvious discomfort. "Until then, I wish you goodbye."

Lifting my hand, I offered a small salute, watching as they turned, his hand sliding to Sindy's backside and squeezing. The man was odious, the last sort of person I'd want around Hilary, but he had huge sway over the London docks, and even I wasn't arrogant enough to think the Hyland name could rule without help. I needed men like Tony supporting my endeavors, ensuring the right shipments got through without the normal customs checks. Keeping wankers like him sweet was important.

Hilary's mewl garnered my attention away from the old man. Smiling, I reached for my glass.

"What's wrong, darling?" I purred. "You're used to being my footrest by now, aren't you?"

She turned her head and fixed me with what she probably thought was a venomous stare. The effect was diluted by the long line of drool gravity helped to the carpet as she moved, alongside those beautiful chiming bells at her tits.

"Oh, you're right, I suppose." Sighing, I drained my champagne, handing it to a nearby member of staff. "It is time we retired."

Lifting my feet from her back, I grasped the leash, still connected to the white collar at her neck, a little tighter, an unspoken reminder of who was in charge—if there could be any doubt. A part of me wondered why she had been so obedient. Hilary could have put up a fight when I stripped her or when I insisted she crawl and beg. I reasoned a lot of the acquiescence was due to sheer embarrassment. She didn't know any of the people assembled, and her humiliation was clearly vast. Maybe she'd reconciled the best way to survive was to keep her head down and do as I said, knowing—accurately—I would make her pay if she refused me.

The other possible cause of her compliance was the tantalizing prospect she might actually have been enjoying the objectification. It would hardly have been the first time. Coupled with my constant teasing, using Hilary this way had made her wet and frantic. Whatever the reason, the fact she hadn't resisted was fucking glorious. It was a wedding that would go down in history.

"Ladies and gentlemen!" I called the room to attention, relishing the way Hilary's head fell at the increased attention. "Let me thank you one and all for attending our special day."

A respectful round of applause broke out around the elegantly furnished space.

"I know I speak for my wife when I say we are eternally grateful."

"Pretty sure she can't say much!" Henry Basinger roared with hilarity at his quip, and several other guests joined him with their laughter.

"That's true," I concurred, tugging Hilary's leash for effect. "So, you'll just have to take my word for it."

"Thanks for inviting us."

I turned my head to witness Bill Foley lifting his glass.

"It's been a hoot."

"I'm glad you agree." I forced a smile in his direction. Foley was the very worst of us—another necessary evil. "Of course, you are all welcome to stay and enjoy yourselves on me, but it's time I took my bride to bed."

A loud cheer rose from the group, along with some crude remarks about what a lucky sod I was.

"I know, I know." Lifting my hands, I received their applause with a grin. "I'm a lucky bastard, but it's time I enjoyed my conjugal rights." Stepping away from my seat, I yanked at Hilary's neck, compelling her to join me. "I hope to see you all again soon." H*opefully, not too soon.*

Flashing a smile at the remaining guests, I encouraged my crawling wife to the door, relishing the sound of her chiming tits before I ordered her to stop and rise to her knees. A very red-faced Hilary met my knowing gaze as I reached down to collect her. Meeting her humbled expression, I helped her to her feet, then lifted her from the ground, throwing her over my right shoulder. I snickered at the shouts that came from the room behind me, patting her bare arse as I turned to leave.

This was the part of the day I'd been looking forward to the most.

Hilary

It had been everything I'd feared and far worse than any of my lewd nightmares. The reality was burned into my psyche for all time. For hours Sean—my new husband—had subjected me to a range of degrading treatments, and he'd done it in front of a roomful of strangers. The church had been awful enough, but to bring me somewhere as sumptuous as this and expose me to more misery—it was too much.

Fresh tears welled in my eyes as he strode from the room, with me thrown ungracefully over his shoulder. His hand stroked my behind, nudging the butt plug still buried there. I squeezed my eyes closed, trying to ignore the demeaning noise the annoying clamps on my nipples insisted on producing. The things barely hurt, but the disparaging sound was enough. No doubt the point was to drill the reality home —I was his wife now, a thing he could strip, bind and torment at will.

"Fortunately for you, I know a back entrance to our suite."

Sean patted my arse again, presumably alluding to a crude comparison of my backside and the hotel. Balling my hands into fists, I considered banging them, along with the chains he'd forced me into, against his body, but there was little point. Acting up would only piss him off, which wasn't the smartest move when he was en route to the place he wanted to fuck me for the first time. He'd also promised me pleasure, and God help me, I didn't want to risk that now. Having endured so much, I merited a few orgasms at least.

"It won't be long now."

I shivered as a rush of cold air passed over me, just about able to make out an outside courtyard. *Oh God.* Closing my eyes, I prayed we'd be gone from here soon. *He was carrying me naked through a courtyard!* I didn't open them again until I noticed the change in air temperature, my scant line of sight confirming we had indeed reentered a building. Taking a flight of steps a few at a time, I wondered how fit Sean was. I was hardly a tiny woman, yet he seemed to manage my weight with little effort.

"Here!" He was gleeful as he swung open a door and marched us inside a carpeted hallway. "Here's our love nest."

I heard the sound of a key turning in a lock, and a moment later, he strode inside. This—*wherever this was*—was to be the site of my next ordeal, but finally, one I'd been looking forward to.

CHAPTER 25: SEAN

Settling her on the bed, I commanded her shackled hands above her head, her knees splaying in silent invitation. There was nothing holding her there, nothing tying her down or compelling her to stay. Her ankles and wrists were in chains, but she could still move, could have left the bed, and made it to the door. I wouldn't have stopped her.

Smiling down at her large imploring eyes, I chuckled to myself. Who was I kidding? Of course, I'd have stopped her, but the point was, Hilary could have chosen to do those things, but she remained silent, save for her ragged breaths, her expression expectant. I'd promised her pleasure on our wedding night, and no doubt, after everything she'd been through today, she thought she deserved it. She was probably right.

"It's been quite a day." I loosened my tie, allowing it to fall around my neck as I gazed down at her. "But we finally did it, beautiful. We're husband and wife."

A strangled whimper bled from her lips, the sound somewhere between agony and ecstasy.

"I know just how you feel, baby." Shrugging out of my jacket, I allowed it to pool at my feet before I unfastened the top button of my shirt. "I've been feeling that way, too." Locking gazes with her intense stare, I moved to the end of the bed, assessing the glistening pussy I was hungry for.

"Now, there's only one more thing we need to do to make it official." I couldn't repress the smile which widened at the tantalizing thought. "It's time to make you mine."

Pressing my palms into the bedding, I climbed over her body. I half expected one of her delicate feet to come flying at me, one last shard of resistance, but as I shifted to straddle her, there was none of the fight I'd witnessed in the past. Gazing down at her face, an urgent desire to kiss her washed over me, and unthinkingly, I slid one finger to her lips, maneuvering the white ball from its place.

"Talk to me." What was this? Was I looking for consent after all the sick things I'd put her through?

"Sean." Hilary's voice was a frantic growl, the noise tightening my balls.

"What?" Brushing my lips over hers, I wanted to fucking devour her. "What do you want?"

Her lids fluttered closed. "I don't even know anymore," she admitted huskily. "I don't know what to think anymore, Sir."

She'd corrected herself without any prompting, the reality pleasing me more than was reasonable.

"You want me." There was no query in my tone, only arrogance a Hyland could master.

"Do you care?" She blinked up at me.

"I said I'd never take you by force." Pressing my palms on either side of her head, my cock ached to be free from its fabric prison and finally impale my bride.

"You said you wouldn't need to."

"And do I?" I probed, lowering my face and inhaling her sweet aroma. Hilary smelled so good, like honey and flowers.

"No." She sounded defeated. "No, Sir. I want you."

"I know you do." No doubt that sounded even cockier than it had in my head, but it didn't matter. She may as well know the man she'd promised to honor and obey. "But I wanted to give you this chance to refuse me, to speak."

Blowing out a breath, her hands rose from the bedding, reaching for my face.

"You're giving me a choice, Sir?"

Her tone was sardonic, but rather than rile me, I smiled.

"Yes. Now's an appropriate time, wouldn't you say?"

"Yes, Sir." Her small fingers grasped the stubble at my chin.

"I meant what I said." Lifting one hand, I captured her fingers and pressed them to my lips. "I'm a sick, possessive bastard, but now that you belong to me, you'll want for nothing, Hilary. I will take care of you."

"I suppose I have to believe you." There was a glimmer of jest in her voice, though it faded as the sentence ended. "I'm your wife."

My lips curled at the way that sounded.

My wife.

She was my wife.

"That's right," I agreed, easing her hands back to the bed behind her. "From now on, we work together, and the first thing we're working on is what I promised you."

"What's that, Sir?" Hilary's eyes flashed with desire, evidence she knew precisely what I was talking about.

"Your needs." Inching down her body, my attention flitted to the clamps still attached to her breasts. "Fuck, you're beautiful." I hadn't intended to say the words out loud, but they'd escaped my lips like a reflex. I was a man of the world, a man who'd bedded a hundred women—each of them as attractive as the next—but I couldn't recall ever craving someone like this.

"Sean." Her hips rose from the bed, brushing against my body, goading me. "Please."

"Do they hurt?" Ignoring her entreaty, I flicked one of the small silver bells, enjoying the chime that had accompanied my evening.

"Not really, Sir." She pulled in a deep breath. "To be honest, I quite like them."

Gazing up the length of her body, I grinned at her audacious reply. It sent fire to my blood.

"What a beguiling woman you are." My brow rose as I continued my journey down her body, planting kisses on her toned stomach before I reached the holy grail. "And how about this pussy of mine?" My heart raced at the accuracy of the question. It was mine, all of her was—*she* was.

"It wants you." Desperation radiated from her throaty tone.

"What was that?" I snapped playfully, lightly smacking her clit as penance.

"Fuck!" Back arching, she groaned. "Sir," she corrected. "It wants you, Sir."

"Good." Settling between her legs, her ankles spread as far as the chains allowed, I gently pressed her inner thighs, splaying her moist pink flesh.

"Holy hell, Hilary." Squeezing my eyes closed, I fought for composure. She was so freaking hot, I could easily lose it then and there.

"Sir?" Her head lifted from the bed.

"It's okay." I shook my head, swallowing down the surging arousal. "Relax, here comes your reward."

"Do I get to come, Sir?" The strain in her voice and the

concern etched into her pretty features reminded me just how long it had been since I'd permitted her release. "Or are you just going to tease me again?"

"Not this time, darling." Licking my lips, I gestured for her to settle back on the bed. "This time, you may come, but I want you to beg me for it first."

Her brow furrowed, lips parting as if she was going to protest, but forcing out a breath, she slumped back against the sheets. That was good enough for me. It was time to feast.

Lapping at her seam, her arousal flooded my senses. The scent of her pussy hardened my cock to the point of discomfort, and her panting mewls goaded me on.

"Delicious," I whispered into her flesh before tonguing her again. I'd tasted Hilary before, but it had been too long since I'd relished the chance.

"Oh, fuck." Her hips rose at my intrusion, rocking their own rhythm as she ground against my face. "Sir, yes."

Normally, I would have punished such crude language from her delectable mouth, but I was too engrossed in the task in hand, too lost in her to consider pausing. Hilary was so turned on, I sensed it wouldn't be long before I pushed her right to the brink, but this time, if she was a good girl, I would topple her over the edge and send her flying. Sliding my hands under her arse cheeks, I pulled her tighter to my face as I devoured her. I had a feeling heaven would be denied to a man like me, but if there was truly such a place, it would be a world where I could eat Hilary for breakfast, lunch, and dinner. As the noises of her choked excitement filled the air, I realized I was already in that place.

I'd found my heaven, after all.

"Don't forget what you need to do," I growled against her

quivering pussy, smiling as her hips rocked, seeking the solace of my mouth.

"Yes, Sir," she panted, moaning as I resumed my meal. "Please." Gasping, she arched her back harder, pushing her sex into my face. "Please, Sir. Please, let me come."

Her words were music to my ears. Had anything ever sounded sweeter?

I considered tormenting her more, contemplated pulling away and leaving her hanging as I took my fill. It was wicked, but I'd done far worse, and it would be exquisite to watch her crestfallen expression as I filled her up. The idea bloomed in my head as I breathed her in, our wet flesh colliding as she sought her hedonism.

"Please, Sir." She sounded frantic, right on the edge of sanity as she waited on my approval, and somewhere deep in my soul, she pulled at whatever passed for my heart.

"Okay," I murmured the consent she craved, turning my attention to her pink, swollen clit. "Come for me."

The moment I wrapped my lips around the sensitive nub, she screeched, her body stilling, fraught with tension as her pleasure erupted.

"Sean!" she screamed as I suckled, groaning as the first waves of desire rolled over her.

Lifting one cheek, I spanked her teasingly, a silent reminder of my expectations, that she wouldn't get away with constantly referring to me the wrong way, but nothing more. In the end, I wouldn't deny her. In the end, the writhing mess of wet, gasping woman was mine.

CHAPTER 26: HILARY

It pained me to admit, but it was the most intense climax of my life. Eyes squeezed closed, head thrust back onto the bed, I clawed at the air as I struggled to take in the oxygen I needed, and still, the hedonism rolled on, robbing me of breath, of words, of any conscious thought. Vaguely aware of Sean moving between my thighs, I forced my eyes open to find him leaning over me, wiping his mouth with the heel of his hand.

"Better?" He arched that damn eyebrow and had the same smirk that had taunted me for so long as his palms landed on either side of my face.

"Yes, Sir." What was the point of denial? I'd deserved that orgasm, and it had been bloody amazing. Now, I wanted the rest of what was owed to me.

"And?"

I could smell the scent of me on his breath, the aroma of my arousal goading, the thought so salacious, my hips rose to grind against his expensive suit.

"Thank you?" I offered, not clear what he expected.

"Well, you're welcome, beautiful." He laughed, lowering to plant a chaste kiss on my lips. "But that wasn't what I meant."

"Sir?"

"What do you want now?" His brow rose, demanding my supplication on this last critical point. "Tell me."

"You, Sir."

I breathed the words, but for the first time, there was a smile on my face. I felt so much better now that I'd come as if the weight of the world had been lifted from my shoulders, and he was right—I *did* want him. I yearned for him to fill me up, to fuck me until I cried out.

"No problem, Hilary." Resting on one palm, he smiled while the other hand unfastened his belt and unzipped what I hoped was caging his raging erection. "You got it."

For one protracted moment, our eyes locked, those brooding blue doors to his soul opening only a fraction to reveal a fragment of the man I just married. Gasping beneath him, I would have begged again to receive him, but the words never came. Suspended in a place between satiation and need, I waited, transfixed by the look of him. Sean fucking Hyland, the man who charged into my life and taken everything. The cruelest, most sadistic man I'd ever encountered—which was saying something among Saul and his friends—but also the man who'd pushed me the lowest and taken me the highest. Sean was that man—the man with my world in his hands.

He splintered the silence with one thrust, his cock finding its way to the place I needed it. A guttural vibration left my throat as he impaled me, my body acknowledging what had been patently true for days. I wanted him. Despite his malicious streak, I desired him, no matter how depraved his demands. As he filled me up, inexplicably, the weight of all those humiliating expectations evaporated.

I was his.

I'd pushed back all I could, refusing to sign his papers until he made me, to no avail. Sean was stronger, faster, and had the clarity of mind that my constant denial had starved me of. I'd had little choice but to find myself here, and I wanted to revel in it, relish this union for everything I could get. Whatever happened between us, Sean had changed me, and whatever feelings I'd harbored for Saul, there was no going back to my old life.

"Hilary." His face lowered to mine, and for the first time, I saw an ounce of feeling in his eyes, a glimmer of ecstatic torment as he slammed into me, a fraction of the emotion he'd subjected me to during my captivity.

Closing my eyes, my senses heightened, everything focusing on the magic he created between my legs. With the damn butt plug still in place, he felt huge inside me, his every movement amplified a dozen times.

"Yes." I wanted more of it. Much more. "Fuck me, Sir."

"Fuck." His lips grazed my shoulder, but his hips commanded a frenzied pace, the friction giving my recently satisfied clit all the impetus it needed to come back to life. "You feel amazing."

I groaned as he nipped my skin, the competing sensations ricocheting in my head, taunting me with his absolute control. Pressing my shackles into the bedding, he controlled my movement, just as he had controlled my welfare and whereabouts from that first night. In his own way, Sean had turned himself into my own personal deity—a man who would be praised and worshiped on demand, a man who played with my pleasure and liberty as if they were nothing but a game.

"Look at me."

My eyes opened at his snarl, locking with his as he

slammed into me again, each lunge breathtaking. I gasped as his hips stilled, every inch of him pressed deep inside.

"Mine." The word reverberated from his lips, ringing in my ears long after it should have faded. "Do you understand?"

"Yes, Sir." Frantic for the sweet friction of his thrusts, I squirmed under him, my hips pushing against his body, yearning for compliance. I was so full—full of burning need, full of him—my body was set to burst into flames if I had to wait much longer.

"Tell. Me." Jaw clenched, he whispered, though his resolve was no less intense.

"I'm yours." Gazing up into those knowing eyes, I almost believed it, nearly fell for the brute who'd taken and subjugated me. It was so easy to believe now that some of the tension had been released, so simple to be lulled by his smooth lies. "All yours, Sir."

Frankly, the ease was terrifying.

"Good girl." With a smile, he withdrew, rising above me like a dark god.

Mewling at the loss, I sucked in my lower lip as I watched him.

"Up on your hands and knees, little one." He gestured for me to move.

Biting back my smile, I scrambled to obey. Of course, Sean wanted to take me from behind. He enjoyed the more carnal depth it offered, but that was okay because I freaking loved it as well. By the time I was in position, he was right behind me, cocooning me as our bodies aligned.

"I like marriage so far." Growling the words into my ear, he grabbed a fist full of my hair and yanked my head back.

I cried out and pushed back against him as I strove for pleasure to assuage the pain.

"Yes." His voice vibrated down my nape, and all at once, he speared me, scattering all other thoughts. "I like it a lot."

"Oh, fuck."

There was no choice but to close my eyes and hang on as he pounded me, the sounds of our bodies slamming together filling the room until all I could hear was our union and the tinkling bells at my nipples, and all I could smell was his spicy cologne. Gripping the sheets, I surrendered, yielding to his cock, to the fist in my hair, and to the relentless drive that had been awoken by lust. I had no idea what would happen between Sean and me, no clue if this would be the first of many scintillating sessions or the only time I'd ever want him, but at this moment, it didn't matter. My only concern was the carnality, the smoldering flame needing to burn, and the sublime connection we created when our bodies fused.

Eventually, his grip relaxed, his fist allowing my head to fall forward, but his brutal rhythm went on, claiming me harder and faster than I'd ever known. Pressing my face into the clean linen, my mind was a fog of indulgence and exhaustion. I wanted more, more of him, but my energy was fading. After a day of ordeals, I scarcely had the strength to stay in position.

"Jesus!"

I sighed as he erupted, smiling with satisfaction. Who would have thought the same man who'd seized and compelled me to be his bride could evoke such a response? Who could have known it was possible? As he shuddered, spilling his cum inside me, that was the truth. The sex had been better than I'd dared to imagine.

"Fuck, Hilary." Sean slapped my arse cheek playfully, the impact draining whatever energy remained in my body as I slumped to my belly.

"I think you just did, Sir," I mumbled into the bedding.

"Yes." Laughing, he collapsed over me, pinioning me into the bed. "Yes, I did, wife."

My toes curled at the way that sounded. I was his wife—his legal spouse—whatever happened.

"You're not going to call me that, are you, Sir?" Twisting my head, I caught his eyes before crashing back to the covers.

"I'll call you whatever I like," he reminded me, rising from my body and encouraging me to roll onto my back. "Just like I'll fuck you whenever I like." He smiled, the twisted smirk that had made me want to rip his handsome features from his face in recent days. "Whenever and wherever."

"Yes, Sir." I was too tired to argue, too weary, and too content. Most of the day had been a maze of misery, but the last hour or so had been the best I could remember.

"You're exhausted." He smiled sympathetically. "I should let you rest."

"Any chance you could remove the plug first, Sir?"

I clenched around the intruder, ashamed to have to ask but knowing it could be now or never. I didn't know when Sean would force the gag back into place. I never knew what he would do next. He was the most intoxicating blend of beautiful and dangerous I'd ever met.

"Feeling full, are we?" Cocking that bloody brow, I could feel the blush crawling over my skin.

"Yes, Sir."

"Okay." He leapt from the bed, then refastened his suit pants. "The answer is yes, but I want to remove it in the shower. Then I can get you cleaned up before I make you all dirty again."

Heart racing, I giggled. Sean was undoubtedly the most perverse man, but on that point, at least, I wasn't complaining. A shower sounded lovely, especially if he planned to let me sleep afterward.

"Thank you, Sir." Shifting to an upright position, I shifted against the plug as the tiny bells at my breasts chimed their merry tune.

"Stay there while I get the shower going." He pointed at me as if I wasn't clear where *there* meant, then turned back in my direction. "I can trust you to wait, can't I?"

"Yes, Sir."

The last hour was probably the first in days I hadn't thought of escape.

"I hope so, Hilary." Moving back to me, he undid the remaining buttons of his shirt, shrugging it from his shoulders to reveal an expanse of muscular chest. "Because I want to trust you." Reaching for me, he ran his fingers under my jaw. "It's been a rough start for us, but now that we're wed, I want that to change. I want a wife as well as a captive."

"As well as?"

His lips twitched at my search for clarification.

"Oh, absolutely," he purred. "You'll always be that woman I chained in the dark, even when I allow you out into the sunshine." His digits tightened on my chin. "Won't you, my love?"

My breath hitched at the change of tack, the edge in his voice an unspoken warning. My new husband was the same bastard who'd plagued me for so long, the same man who'd reveled in my utter debasement. I shouldn't let the sizzling sex blind me to that fact or be taken in by the sudden rush of hormones.

"Yes." Ultimately, my answer was barely a whisper, the word almost lost. "Yes, Sir."

"That's right." Bending to me, his face lowered until he was only inches away. "There's my good little wife."

I clenched at his patronizing tone. There was no way it should have been so hot. "I promise I'll stay right here, Sir."

Fluttering my eyelashes, I might even have meant it. "While you run the shower."

"That's a good answer." His lips grazed over my mouth, teasing me with the kiss he rarely permitted. Smiling, his gaze drilled into mine. "Because you should know the door is locked, and there's nowhere you can run, little lady. I have moles everywhere, people who report to me, and none of them will be your friend."

My heart hammered at the menace in his tone, but I fought to control it. Sean had coerced me with threats long enough. I'd done what he asked for—I'd become his wife. It was time to remind him of that.

"I understand."

Rising to my knees, I returned the caress he'd initiated, nibbling his lower lip as his hand lowered to my waist.

"What are you playing at?" He chuckled teasingly, his palm lowering to my backside and swatting it.

"I was just thinking…" I started, planting a trail of kisses on his jaw.

"Oh, yeah?"

He was trying to stay firm and in control, but the huskiness in his voice gave him away, and just like that, he gave me what I wanted—a lead-in to the next conversation.

"What are you thinking?"

"If I'm yours, Sir, then you must be mine as well."

"Is that right?" This time, he laughed, the fire dancing in his eyes, stoking the flames still searing inside me.

"Yes," I breathed between kisses. "That's right. Mine to kiss, mine to fuck, and…" Gazing up at him with a smile, I lifted my shackled wrists around his neck. "Mine to claim." Pressing my mouth to his, I swooped, finally taking the tenderness I needed.

CHAPTER 27: SEAN

The darkness enveloped me, shrouding me in an odd sense I'd rarely known. My lips curled as the source of the solace sprung to mind—*contentment*. Stretched out in the shadows with my new wife, I was content. Who'd have known all it would take to find such bliss was one hot submissive wife and The Prince of Wales suite at The Ritz. Life was certainly amusing in its haze of contradictions.

Breathing in the smell of her hair, I pulled her closer, wrapping my arms around her. Hilary stirred, letting out a breathy mewl that threatened to rouse my cock once more, but it didn't take long for the sounds of her restful sleep to fill the silence again. This was definitely better than keeping her bound in another room. I liked holding her, enjoyed having her with me, and after the sensual shower we'd both relished, a soak which involved another climatic orgasm being ripped from her desperate body, I was happy just to have her close. Sleep, it seemed, was as elusive as contentment had once been, but closing my eyes, it didn't matter. We had no plans for the next day except more of this. I would fuck and hold my new bride as often as it pleased us both.

I was on the verge of permitting slumber to overcome me when I heard the telltale noises of steps outside the suite door, heavy feet on the luxurious carpet. My heart picked up its pace, sending adrenaline racing and splintering any hope of rest. Who would be wandering the halls of the hotel at this time of night? The Ritz was one of the most expensive hotels in the country, and this suite, one of its most exclusive rooms, so the footfall outside wasn't high frequency.

Lifting my head from the pillow, I eased away from Hilary, ensuring she hadn't woken before I strained my ears, listening for anything further. For a moment, stony silence swirled past my eardrums, nearly convincing me I'd imagined the whole thing until a shuffle from outside in the corridor garnered my attention again. I was on my feet, creeping out of the bedroom to the main entrance in a heartbeat. Pressing my head against the door, I focused on what was coming from beyond it.

Tread. Definitely tread, from one, maybe more pairs of shoes. My every instinct told me something was very wrong with this scenario. People didn't linger outside lavish suites, and if it did happen to be a member of staff, they would have knocked by now, apologizing profusely for the inconvenience.

"Is this the room?"

The unmistakable sound of a man's muted voice met my ear, and straightening, I stared at the door. Who the hell was he? Who would be here at this time? I didn't wait for the answers to hit me in the face, turning and dashing back to my clothes. Pulling on my pants, I found the gun I'd kept stashed away in my overnight bag for emergencies. I wasn't sure what was going on, but I'd been a Hyland long enough to trust my instincts—and each one sounded alarm bells.

"Sean?" Half-asleep, her voice floated from the bed, and in the shadows, I could just make out her silhouette as she rose to one elbow. "Sir, what's wrong?"

My lips twitched at the way she addressed me, despite the dread escalating in the pit of my stomach.

"Shhh." Striding to the bed, I lowered my voice. "I'm not sure, but I think there's someone outside."

"What?" She leaned closer to me. "I don't understand."

"I said shhh." I was near enough to whisper. "Stay here. I'm going to check it out."

"Sir."

She sounded fraught, a tone I wasn't used to unless I was the cause of her anxiety. The thought some other wanker could induce those feelings was less than satisfying. Whatever our genesis, Hilary was my wife now. It was my responsibility to take care of her, to protect her.

"It's okay." I tried to reassure, but the knotting tension inside assured me I'd failed. "Just stay here. I won't let anything happen to you." On that point, at least, I was resolved.

Spinning on my heel, I reached for the weapon stashed in my pocket. The safety might be on, but it would only take a matter of seconds to rectify that situation. I was about halfway to the suite door when I heard the unmistakable sound of a key in the lock. I was sure my heart stopped beating altogether. Why was there a key in the lock? I had the only key to the suite, and I'd instructed the hotel staff to stay away unless I needed assistance. Paralyzed with uncertainty, I stood in the near darkness, watching as the door inched open. Grasping my weapon, ready to fire, I pointed it at the door before it fully opened.

"Think again, fucker." As if the gun had broken an invisible spell, my cocky bravado was back with a vengeance. "I have a gun directed right at you. Do yourself a favor and walk away."

"Not until I get what I came for."

Straightening, I was surprised at the viciousness of the response. Usually, the kinds of guys who did these jobs were all mouth and no trousers. It only took one gentle push to topple them into oblivion, but this guy was different. The mettle in his voice was startling.

"And what's that, arsehole?" Gripping the gun, I moved closer. "You know who you're dealing with, don't you?"

"That would be Hilary Mantle."

From behind me in the bedroom, Hilary's gasp was audible, the sound hardening my will.

"There's nobody here by that name." My heart pounded as what sounded like at least two other pairs of shoes bundled into the room. "The only woman here is Hilary Hyland, and she belongs to me."

The overhead light flickered on, the scene unraveling in front of me like a terrible movie. There were more than half a dozen men I didn't recognize dressed in black, brandishing weapons, but the biggest shock was yet to come. Assessing the entourage, my gaze landed on the one closest to me, and his face was instantly familiar.

"Morrison." I gritted my teeth at the unwelcome sight.

"Hyland." He nodded in my direction, his gaze scanning the suite behind me before he gestured to one of the ogres at his rear.

It all happened so fast. Time, which had protracted in the shadows, sped up with the signal, and five of the men came at me with vexing agility.

"Stay back!" I warned, squeezing the trigger, but one of

them was already behind me, wrestling me to the ground. By the time the gun fired, the bullet hit the ornate ceiling, chipping the priceless décor.

I was vaguely aware of Morrison striding past, of the horror that filled me as he headed to the bedroom—the place where my wife was waiting—but pinned down by numerous pairs of brutal hands, a number of which were attempting to throw punches in my direction, there was nothing I could do to stop him.

"Hilary!" I screamed, straining to turn around and see if she was okay, but the cumbersome oafs holding me down gave me little hope of that.

"Sean!"

I could hear the panic in her voice, trepidation twisting inside at the sound.

"What's happen—" She never finished that sentence, and though I couldn't see why, I could take an educated guess.

Morrison.

"Hilary."

Even I was forced to acknowledge the relief in his voice.

"Oh my God, Hilary, are you okay?"

"Saul?" Shock resonated in her tone. "Wh-What are you doing here?"

It was a fucking good question, but one Morrison only sniggered at.

"I've come for you, silly. Isn't it obvious?" He chuckled. "I've come to rescue you."

CHAPTER 28: HILARY

This couldn't be happening. I refused to acknowledge it. After all the days of waiting, thinking of Saul, praying for him to come, for someone—*anyone*—to drag me away from Sean's clutches, he decided to make an entrance now? Now that I'd been forced to endure the torment that was my alleged wedding day, and now that Sean and I had finally satiated the desire brimming between us. This was the moment my old lover decided to show up—seriously?

"For me?" I shook my head, gripping the covers closer to my chest. Despite the endless binds Sean had employed during our special day, I was unfettered and free to recoil away from Saul. "Why?"

"Why?" Saul's eyes widened. "What do you mean, why? This arsehole took you from right under my nose." He turned, gesturing into the other room.

Pulling the sheets off the bed, I slid from it and wandered the short distance to see what was happening. Sean was held down by numerous men wielding weapons, his bloodied face evidence of the welcome he'd received. My brow furrowed, confusion warring inside me. I'd wanted to see Sean suffer for so long, to see pain etched into his features, to see him impotent and powerless. I'd fantasized about it in those long, dark hours alone, bound to the chair, but the scene playing out now wasn't half as satisfying as I'd anticipated. Little in the way of glee rose at the sight of Sean's helplessness, and even less excitement was inspired by Saul.

Shifting my focus back to him, my gaze traveled over his concerned expression. *Saul.* I thought I'd been falling in love with him, had lofty aspirations of a life together, but staring at him, there was a disconnect. It wasn't that I loved Sean—far from it, though I had noticed fleeting moments of tenderness in his touch—it was more, whatever feelings had burgeoned for Saul had faded. All those times I'd longed for him, desired for him to be my savior had amounted to nothing, and with the nothing came a new, stark reality.

I was on my own. I might have been embroiled with The Syndicate, and that association could well have been the cause of my abduction, but apparently, I wasn't entwined enough to warrant rescue. When Dalton's girlfriend, Delilah, had been taken captive by Sean's uncle, Saul and the others had moved heaven and earth to find her, to free her from Zander's ugly grip, but for some reason, I didn't warrant the same salvage. Regarding Saul now, it all flooded back, that sense of rejection stinging all the harder as I was forced to acknowledge it.

"Hilary?" Saul inched toward me, one hand rising toward my face.

"Where have you been?" There was venom in my voice, and briefly, I noticed him register it, the hurt flickering in his eyes.

"What do you mean?"

"I mean, where have you been all this time, Saul?" Anger

simmered in my veins, my hands grasping the fabric closer to my chest. "I've been gone for…" Hesitating, I tried to recall just how long Sean had held me. "I don't even know how long, but days, Saul, maybe weeks. Where were you?" My voice croaked with emotion, all those hours of lonely despair peaking until finally, the question I'd wanted to ask flew from my lips.

"Where were you when I needed you?"

"I-I was looking for you." He faltered, an expression of powerlessness appearing on his face. I'd never seen such uncertainty from him before, and it might have been amusing had it not been so infuriating.

"You could have found me in a couple of days," I spat at him. "Even I know enough about The Syndicate to know that. Why didn't you come before?" Shaking my head, I refused to acknowledge the tears burning in my eyes.

"I'm sorry." His hand, which had been hovering in the air between us, fell to his side. "You're right. I should have come sooner."

"You're damn right you should have come." The fury had focused me, making it easier to convey my resentment. I deserved more, and it was time Saul knew it.

"Are you okay?" Saul stepped forward again, his eyes moist with emotion. "Did he hurt you?"

Inhaling, I wanted to fucking laugh.

"Hurt me?" My tone dripped with disdain. "What do you think he's been doing with me all this time? Treating me to five-star luxury?"

Saul's gaze stretched past me, landing on Sean.

"What have you done to her, you bastard?" Pacing in his direction, Saul pointed a finger at him. "If you've so much as hurt a hair on her head, I swear, I'll fucking kill you."

A heavy silence stretched out around us, broken only by

the dark, dry laughter of my husband. I shivered, glancing from Saul to Sean.

"Well, ain't that sweet?" Sean's sardonic tone drifted through the air, his hilarity punctuated only by the fist which walloped his nose.

I flinched at the dull thud, my insides twisting as blood poured from Sean's nose. Two more of Saul's guys hovered over him, brandishing guns.

"Don't hurt him," I ordered the mean-looking guy leaning over Sean, fist already pulling back for another shot. It took a moment for me to realize he was actually Connor Reilly—one of Saul's closest allies at The Syndicate. "Just leave him alone."

Connor lifted his head, those green eyes boring into me.

"Seriously?" Saul's attention shot back to me. "You're defending him—the man who took you?"

"Yes." I lifted my chin, the reality suddenly hitting me. I *was* defending him. Why was that? "Listen, Sean is no fucking hero. He's a swine, and he's treated me like shit."

"Charming," Sean sniggered from the floor, though I noted there was no protest, no attempt to defend himself.

"Well, it's true." I shot a look in his direction, able to tell him how I felt for the first time. "And you know it."

"Hey, I'm not denying it." A smirk lit up his face, despite the blood and the fist still hovering above it. "I'm an arsehole."

"Right." Blowing out a breath, I was pleased he at least accepted it. "But whatever he's done, he's never punched me." I glanced back to Saul, imploring him to see reason. "You're as bad as each other, Saul. You take other people and treat them like dirt. You use them, abuse them, and don't care who gets in the way." Wiping my tears with the heel of my hand, my jaw clenched. "And this is what you get." I gestured toward myself, abruptly aware of how naked I was beneath the sheet. "This is what you get when you live this way—I'm the collateral damage."

"She's right." Sean chuckled. "You know she's right, Morrison."

Saul's gaze narrowed at his rival's accusation. "Fuck you, Hyland."

Sean's grisly laughter echoed from the other room again.

"No thanks, you're really not my type, and anyway, I have a beautiful new wife to take care of those needs."

Saul's mouth closed, his focus drilling back into me.

"So, you're married now?"

"I didn't really have much of a choice." I didn't like his tone or the inference that Sean had somehow been my selection. Frankly, I hadn't even wanted marriage. "I'm not sure if you know, but I was fucking kidnapped," I sneered lowly, the rage that had just started to dissipate knotting in my chest.

Saul pulled in a deep breath, his gaze rising to the ceiling.

"So, yeah." I wanted to shift my hands to my hips to show my defiance. "I'm married. Are you happy now? Have you got what you came for?"

"I came here for you." His voice was heavy as he regarded me again. "To take you away from him, but if you're telling me you want to stay, then I guess I'm too late."

"That's right." Sean's unhelpful sneer cut through the tension. "Too late, Morrison—that's exactly what you are."

"Oh, fuck you, Hyland!" Saul hollered at him. "No one was fucking talking to you."

"Well, tough shit." Sean chuckled, spitting his blood onto the carpet beside him. "I'm part of the equation now."

"Yeah, don't I fucking know it?" Saul snarled.

"Oh, shut up, both of you!" I screamed, stomping my foot.

"I want some time to think, and all you're doing is calling each other names. You're like a couple of kids."

"Looks like you need to train your wife a little better, Hyland…"

I tensed at Saul's quip.

"What the hell, Saul?" I paced toward him, jabbing my finger into his chest. This version of The Syndicate's leader was nothing like the man I'd been dating, nothing like the considerate, tender lover I'd missed. Whether it was all only cocky bravado in front of Sean, I didn't like it. "Who do you think you're talking about?"

Saul's gaze slid back to me. "You know what I mean."

"No!" I snapped. "No, I don't. You're not the man I thought you were, Saul, not the one I was happy with…" My voice trailed away as I blinked away the remaining tears. "I can't believe this."

"Okay, I'm sorry." Saul sighed. "This hasn't exactly gone the way I expected."

"No shit," I muttered. "What did you think was going to happen? You'd just bowl in here on our wedding night, and everything would be forgiven?" Swallowing back on the rising tide of emotion, I realized this conversation was going nowhere. Whatever Saul's objective had been was irrelevant. I was fed up with these men bossing me around.

"Look, just let Sean up, and maybe we can all talk like adults."

"Talk?" Sean snorted from beneath Connor. "These guys just busted in on our wedding night and pounded the shit out of me. The last thing I want to do is talk. They can kiss my arse!"

Stumbling back, I perched on the end of the bed. It was going to be a long night.

"Maybe you deserved some of this, Sean." It was a relief to

be frank with him for a change without fear of repercussion. "I meant what I said. You're both as bad as the other." I glanced down at Sean, my gaze trailing over his semi-naked body. "You've both treated me badly and taken me for granted."

I watched as Sean and Saul locked gazes. There were no words of complaint.

"I've had enough of this." Rising from the bed, I stomped toward the huge wardrobe in the corner. Sean had already told me clothing was waiting for me, and this was as good a time as any to see for myself.

"What are you doing?" In the end, it was Saul who asked as I threw back the wooden door and examined the possibilities.

"I'm getting dressed," I answered, without turning back to acknowledge him.

"Hey, no way!" That was Sean's voice. Turning, I was actually grateful to see Connor holding him down. "I never said you could get dressed."

"Tough." Tugging a pair of dark yoga pants from the hanger, I found a blouse and headed into the en suite bathroom. "I'm fed up with you telling me what to do."

Dropping the sheet, I pulled on the pants before slipping into the cool blouse. It felt good to be dressed again, to be on my feet again, thinking for myself. Now that Sean had dampened the fire blazing in my core, I could finally concentrate. Everything seemed clearer.

Moving back into the bedroom, I found Saul waiting, his hands in his pockets.

"What's your plan?" He sounded neither judgmental nor authoritative.

"I'm leaving." I threw him a cursory glance before I delved into the bottom of the wardrobe, retrieving a pair of slip-on shoes. "If you're asking where I'm going, I'm not telling you." Hell, I didn't even know myself.

"You're going fucking nowhere."

We both turned at Sean's snarl, Saul glancing back at me with a sigh.

"Want me to keep him busy while you leave?"

My attention slipped from one lover to the other. There had been times in the last few weeks I'd cared for them both and others when I wanted to punch them, but I appreciated the offer. If I was to have any chance of escaping Sean's clutches, I had to get ahead of him.

"Thank you, yes."

Sliding my feet into the black leather, I walked to Saul, rising to my tiptoes to plant a kiss on his chin. He wasn't a bad man at heart, I knew that, but like Sean, he wasn't a good man, either. He wasn't good enough for me.

"I need some space."

"I understand." Saul's jaw tightened as his gaze pierced me. "You know where I am if you need me."

"Thank you, Saul." Breathing in the familiar scent of his aftershave, I nodded, ignoring the profanity spilling from Sean. Taking one last look at Sean before I strode away, I didn't stop to talk to him, didn't want to hear his protests. He'd taken so much from me already—they both had. By the time I'd reached the door to the suite, I was resolved.

This was my time.

I was moving on.

CHAPTER 29: SEAN

"No!" Watching as the door slammed shut was like a knife to my heart. "Hilary!"

"Looks like you should have treated her a little better, Hyland." The dark-haired guy who'd been throwing the punches sneered in my direction, one of the others waving a gun in my face. "Doesn't seem like she wants you, after all."

"Fuck you!" I spat the blood still swilling in my mouth at him, relishing the way he recoiled, disgusted. "Get the fuck off me."

"No way." Morrison's voice came from behind me.

Turning, I saw him walk into the room. The man looked thoroughly dejected, and at any other time, his expression would have made me gleeful. "You heard the lady, she needs some space, and we're going to make sure she gets it."

"How fucking gallant of you," I mocked. My head ached from the earlier onslaught, rounds of punches I hadn't been prepared for, coupled with the impact of the floor as I'd fallen. "You know I'll get her back, right? You know she's my wife?"

"Ever heard of a divorce lawyer?" Morrison fired back. "I know a good one. I'll help her out."

"You'll stay the fuck away from her." Rage roared from somewhere deep inside. "Stay away from my wife."

"Listen to him." The prick, still holding me down with the help of his chums, rolled his eyes. "You'd almost think she actually consented to the arrangement."

Saul laughed, the sound twisting inside me. How dare he be fucking happy? If he hadn't barged in here in the middle of the night, I would have been happy, content with the only woman I'd ever committed anything to.

"Doesn't look like she consented to be with you either, huh?" Ultimately, I fell back on the oldest trick in the book, deflecting my own pain by lashing out at someone else—the cause of my misery. "I don't see Hilary leaving with you."

Slipping his hands in his pockets, he stood over me.

"No," he ceded, the pain of that reality glimmering briefly in his eyes. "In the end, she didn't choose either of us."

"She already chose me," I growled, reminding him yet again of the recent developments in Hilary's life. Only a matter of hours earlier, she'd stood at the altar and consented to love, honor, and obey me.

"None of us believe she had a choice in that," Saul sniggered as if I'd just spun him a yarn.

"You'd better believe she had a choice in the consummation!" I spat, just as one of the burlier guys over me shifted. Seizing the only chance I had since I landed on my back, I shoved him back, knocking the gun away before turning just in time to avoid another punch from the dark-haired one. Kicking one of the others in the face, I made it to my feet. "She fucking begged me for it."

"You're a real son-of-a-bitch, Hyland." Morrison shook

his head as the dark-haired one grabbed me from behind. He was stronger than he looked. "She was never yours to take."

Pulling at the hold the stranger had on me, I eyeballed Morrison as he stepped toward me.

"And in taking her, you fucked both our chances."

"Speak for yourself," I retorted. "She's still my wife."

"Oh, change the fucking record," whined one of the others, pointing his gun at me. "If you were so damn special to her, she didn't seem that upset to leave you."

I turned to meet his piggy little eyes. "You don't know anything about it," I shouted, shrugging away from the idiot trying to hold me back. "None of you do."

"Cover the door." Saul nodded to his men, his gaze sliding back to me as three of them moved to the door of the suite. "You're not going anywhere, Sean. You might as well get used to it."

"Oh, yeah?" Bravado racing through my blood like adrenaline, I shoved the dark-haired one away and lurched for my gun. It had been just out of my reach the whole time but incapacitated on the floor, there'd been no opportunity to grab it. "What are you going to do about it?"

"We're going to fucking shoot you, you moron." The one behind me laughed, wrestling the weapon from my hands.

"Hey!" Spinning on my heel, I lunged at him, but before I could grapple for the gun, another two imbeciles were on me, the barrels of their guns pointed at my head.

"I wouldn't if I were you." There was no glee in Morrison's voice, only a weary sense of resignation. "We will kill you, Hyland."

"Just like you killed my uncle." I turned, swiveling between the weapons.

"That's right." Saul pressed his lips together. "I don't take pleasure in it, but you Hylands just keep sticking your noses in my business."

Snorting, I tried to think, but the hammering in my head was making it impossible to focus.

"You're just going to let her walk away?" I gestured toward the door. "Just let her leave in the middle of the night with no money and nowhere to go."

"She could go home." Morrison's brow furrowed.

"Hardly," I muttered. "She knows both of us will go straight there."

"I won't," he assured me with just a little too much insistence. "I will respect her wishes."

"Good for you," I grunted. "I won't. I'll do whatever it takes to take care of her while you just allowed her to roam free on the streets of this shitty city."

"She'll probably just get a room somewhere." Morrison ignored my bait. "She'll be safe. Hilary knows this city."

"Who are you trying to kid?" I asked, inching closer while the guns pressed into the sides of my head. "She doesn't have any fucking money, you prick. Hilary's about as savvy as Mickey Mouse. How do you think I picked her up so easily?"

Morrison gulped, a flicker of concern flashing in his eyes.

"You know I'm right, don't you?" I could sense triumph on this one small matter. "She'll never survive out there on her own."

His gaze flitted to the dark-haired guy. "He might have a point, Connor."

"Fucking great," his friend replied. "And you couldn't have thought of this before you let her leave?"

My lips twitched at the friction between them.

"Listen, you can cuff me, whatever you need to do, but let's get out there and find her together. We both care about her, right?" It was a dangerous strategy, soliciting the help of my biggest rival—the same man who'd murdered my uncle in cold blood—but these were desperate times, and based on his faltering expression, it might just work. "She can't have got far."

"Maybe you're right." Morrison's hand lifted to his temple as if he couldn't believe he agreed with me.

"For fuck's sake, Saul." The dark-haired one, Connor, removed the tip of his weapon from my head. "Really?"

"Tie him up." Morrison directed to one of the guys standing near him. "We're getting out of here, and Hyland's coming with us."

CHAPTER 30: HILARY

Breathing in the dank London air, exhilaration bloomed in my veins. Sure, I was wandering around in uncomfortable, unseasonal clothes that weren't mine. I was cold and exhausted, and I hadn't even started to process the shit I'd been through in the last few days, but none of that mattered—I was free! Free from Sean and Saul in one fell swoop. It was a work of genius!

Hugging my arms around my chest, I ignored the chill and the endless tap, tap, tapping of the new shoes against the concrete. They weren't my style, and I wasn't crazy about the way they rubbed the back of my feet, but I wasn't complaining. I was clothed and away from all the fucked-up men in my life. Sure, I knew I was vulnerable out here on my own, especially since I had no cash with me, no phone, and not even the key to my own place, but at least whatever happened would be down to me. Glancing down the long road of Piccadilly, I wondered what my options were. I could go to the police, seek some sort of sanctuary there, but was I really prepared to snitch on my former lover and employer? If I went to the authorities, they would ask all sorts of questions, and no matter how much crap Saul had put me through, I didn't want that. Whatever I felt for him, he'd been good to me in the past—all his guys had—and I couldn't repay that with such flagrant treachery.

"Are you lost, darling?"

I froze at the foreign voice, peering into the darkness of Green Park to find a toothless man staring at me.

"Oh, I'm fine, thanks," I intended to hurry down the path, but from out of the shadows, another man appeared, blocking my route.

"You're sure?" This one had a crooked smile, but he smelled just like the first, the pungent aroma of urine and body odor wafting past my nostrils. "We don't mind helping you out, lass."

"Really?" Flustered, I stumbled back, meaning to turn back toward the hotel, but to my horror, another two men were already waiting for me. "Thank you for the kind offer, but no."

Eyeing the opposite side of the enormous road, I considered making a dash for it. There was no traffic at this time of night and seemingly no other pedestrians around to assist me. I had nothing to lose.

"Don't do that," the first one cajoled. "We won't bite ya. We only want to talk."

"I thought you wanted to help?" Why was I engaging the guy? The smell of him and his friends alone was making me nauseous.

"Help and talk," one of them behind me clarified. By the time I spun on my heel, another one had manifested from the damp sidewalk, creating a dreadful circle around me. "We don't get many beautiful women passing this way. Why don't you come into the park and chat?"

"No, thank you." My heart raced as I turned, eyeing the

awful men. They were filthy, and though I had no way of knowing what their true intentions were, the dark light shining in their eyes promised brutal, heinous things. I had to get away. "I have to get home. My boyfriend will be waiting."

The one who'd first stepped out of the shadows snorted. "What kind of boyfriend would allow you to walk down here on your own?"

"That's none of your business."

"I think she's lying." One of their voices floated past my ears, and I jumped at his proximity, dread escalating in my belly. "I don't think there is a boyfriend."

"Please." Panic clawed at my insides. I hadn't just escaped from one traumatic situation to land myself in another one on the street. "Just leave me be."

"I don't think so, darling." He was right behind me, his revolting odor attacking my nostrils with fresh ferocity. "I think we're going to play with you for a while."

"No!" Skipping away from him, I nearly ran into one of the others. The circle they'd created grew smaller while I stood and watched. "Stop it! Help me, someone, help me!"

Twisting around to determine my position, the answer to my plea smacked me right in the face. These repulsive strangers weren't going to go without a fight, and there wasn't a soul around to hear me cry.

Saul

It only took Adams a few minutes to bind Hyland's hands behind his back, then we were on the move. Leaving his plush suite, I ensured he was shielded by my men as we slipped out of the back entrance, the same way we'd entered. The décor at The Ritz might be first class, but its security was seriously lacking. We were heading into the expanse of Green Park when I heard it, the sound tightening the tension in my gut until I nearly doubled over.

"No!" A female voice cried out from the edge of the park. I knew that voice. "Stop it! Help me, someone, help me!"

"That's Hilary!" Hyland took the words right out of my mouth. He charged past Connor, knocking him out of the way, running toward her voice.

"Fuck!" I was after him in a heartbeat, not only because I'd made a promise to Hilary but because there wasn't much he could do with his hands bound. "Come on, Connor."

Glancing behind me, I caught sight of them running in the same direction. Heart pounding, I focused my attention on catching up with Hyland. He was already at the perimeter of the park, leaping the hurdle the metal fence presented.

"Get your fucking hands off her!" Sean's holler echoed around the night sky, and as I leapt after him, it was easy to see what—*who*—had rattled his cage. A collection of what looked like homeless vagabonds were crowding Hilary, one of them pawing at her chest.

"Oh, yeah." The stranger's ugly face contorted into a sneer. "What are you gonna do about it, armless?"

"He's not going to do anything," I concurred, reaching for my weapon. "But my friends and I, we're a whole different proposition."

Connor and the others advanced on the collection of groping vagrants and shoved their guns into their backs.

"Back away, arsehole," Connor snarled to the one in front

of him, jabbing him with the weapon as he turned to face him. "Give the lady some space."

"Hilary." Pushing past another, I found her wide-eyed and terrified. "Are you okay?"

Gasping, her focus flitted from Sean to me. "I'm okay," she told me, but I wasn't convinced by her trembling voice.

"Didn't you hear him?" Hyland's voice was vicious. "Back the fuck away."

Gradually, once enough weapons were pushed into their faces, the tramps seemed to give up the fight. Backing away, they slunk into the night, disappearing into the shadows of the park.

"Hilary." Hyland shook his head, his eyes narrowing despite his restrained position. "What the hell happened?"

"They just came out of nowhere." Her expression crumpled at his approach. "I didn't know what to do."

"Just as well we were here, huh?" I arched a brow in her direction, and her gaze darted to meet it.

"Yes." I could see it pained her to concede the point. "Thank you, all." She paused, wrapping her arms around her body. "Hang on, why are you all here?"

"That doesn't sound much like gratitude." Hyland pressed himself up against her, and I watched as her chin rose, meeting his eyes. For the first time, I saw the two of them together and had a sense of the chemistry they'd carved. The reality was unsettling. I'd never made any real commitment to Hilary, but I'd thought we were headed on a journey together. To see her with another man was jarring, especially one as ruthless as Hyland.

"I'm sorry," she murmured.

"What?" His brow rose as if he was prompting her.

Staring in silence, I felt the tangible shift in the

atmosphere. Hilary's face heated in a blush as her gaze fell to his chest.

"Sir."

The word was barely audible.

"I'm sorry, Sir."

My eyes widened. Connor's gaze burned into me as though he wanted an explanation.

"Better." Hyland's expression softened. "But just wait until I'm unfettered. You'll pay for this, young lady."

"Yes, Sir." Her feet shifted at his side, weight moving from one to the other.

I expected to see fear shining in her eyes, but when my gaze traveled up her body, I was bewildered to see a small smile on her lips. Could it be she actually enjoyed his threats, let alone his attention? It was difficult to breathe as that idea resonated.

"You haven't answered my question?" She turned, catching my eyes before her gaze slipped around my men. "Where are you all going?"

"We're taking Hyland prisoner." The answer came to me in a split second, and even as it left my lips, I knew why I'd said it. I had promised her the space to think, to get away, then in a matter of moments, I'd changed my mind, pursuing her. "And since we found you, we're taking you with us."

She and Hyland locked gazes with me.

"What?" Hyland asked, though I could see the same query burning in her eyes.

"You heard me," I snapped, tired of explaining myself to this prick. He'd been nothing but a pain in the arse since he'd landed back in the country. "Connor, let's get them to the cars."

"Sure." Lips curling, Connor nodded over Hyland's shoulder, his weapon already pushed into my rival's back.

Turning to the road, I caught sight of our vehicles parked on the deserted street. With our waiting drivers, we would be away in a matter of moments.

"You'll pay for this, Morrison." Hyland narrowed his gaze. "You have no fucking right."

"You made it my right." Stepping past Hilary, I pushed myself in his face. "When you helped yourself to my girlfriend."

"Gonna make her choose, are you?"

I wanted to rip the smug, self-satisfied smirk from his self-righteous face.

"That's right," I roared in his face. "I'm going to make her choose, and we already both know which way the dice will fall, don't we, Hyland?"

"Oh, yeah." He chuckled, even as Connor encouraged him forward.

Sean Hyland—the man whose desire had brought down the whole tower of cards.

"I know exactly who she'll opt for. You lose, Morrison. You lose."

The End.

Devour Hyland's Obsession *for* the next sizzling installment of Hilary and Sean's twisted love affair!

Read the introduction to the book now...

HYLAND'S OBSESSION

Hyland's Obsession
(A Rage and Revenge Novel):
A Dark Mafia Dark Necessities Romance.

Book Three
By
Felicity Brandon

Copyright © 2021 by Felicity Brandon

Prologue: Sean Hyland

Glancing over to the place Hilary huddled beside me, anxiety twisted inside. I loathed to see her so fearful, unless of course, I was the one inspiring the fear. I resented the power Morrison and his cronies exerted. Her large eyes rose to meet my glare before quickly, she looked away. Guilt flickered in her gaze, an acknowledgement of how we'd both landed ourselves in this mess. This was Hilary's fault. Even though the moron Morrison had been the one to storm our wedding night—it was all on her. I should have known he would try something like this, should have anticipated his next move, but foolishly, I expected better from my new wife. She'd been the one who'd wandered out into the night, alone and without a penny to her name. She'd been the one who'd got herself into trouble within the first few minutes of her so-called freedom.

Lowering my head, I recalled how I'd raced to her. It didn't matter that my hands were bound, in that split second, I acted only on instinct. The urge to save her from the grubby hands of the vagrants, the need to protect what belonged to me.

What was mine.

"Sean." Her voice carried softly over the backseat. "Sir."

My lips curled as she addressed me the right way. It didn't matter that we were both prisoners of my greatest enemy, Morrison, the same man who'd put a bullet in my uncle's brain. My influence over her was still strong. Robust enough to compel the important word from her lips.

"What?" My response was intentionally terse.

"I'm sorry." Her voice was a strained whisper. "I didn't mean for any of this to happen."

I turned to her, the emotion in her tone tugging at what little remained of my heart. "You will pay for the mistakes you made tonight." I didn't want there to be any misunderstanding. "But it's okay. I'm here. You're safe."

Though *safe* was a relative term. I was the man who had snatched her from a dank London street, had taken her for my own, tormented her and compelled her into marriage. I was no hero, but I *was* her husband. Hilary was mine, I would never let any harm come to her. I'd never let her go.

"Aww, ain't that sweet." The dark-haired guy in the front seat, Connor, who'd repeatedly driven his fist into my face in our suite at The Ritz smirked. "He's going to keep her safe."

From across the back seat, Saul Morrison glared in my direction. "He'll be doing nothing unless I approve it first."

Fury simmered in my blood. To think the insidious moron who slaughtered my uncle in cold blood was now calling the shots filled me with rage. I hated the guy more than I'd ever loathed anyone, but in the short term at least, he was right. I was bound. Hilary was bound, and we were both on our way to the headquarters of Morrison's organization, The Syndicate, where no doubt he intended to *interrogate* me further.

My jaw tightened at the unpleasant thought. I'd been around long enough to know what went on during those sessions, having been privy to many of them myself over the years before I lived in the south of France. I didn't fear pain, but I certainly didn't seek it. A face like mine looked better on the front page than at the end of a fist, but more worrying was Hilary. Turning back to her, our gazes met. Morrison had foolishly shoved us both into the back seat together, a mistake I would never have made in his place, but one that afforded me a few further precious moments with my bride.

"It's okay." I whispered, but even I could hear the strain in my voice, the nagging doubt that maybe it wasn't. Maybe it never would be again.

What would they do to her now that I'd compelled her to take her wedding vows? Would Morrison consider her soiled because she was mine? Would he hurt *her*, as well?

Anger swelled inside until my shoulders trembled and I was forced to push out a long breath.

"Sean."

Hilary leaned toward me, mouthing the word. Normally,

I'd have not looked favorably upon the use of my name, but for once, I was soothed by it. Consoled by its intimacy. She was my wife and she needed me. If truth be told, I needed her, as well. Our few blissful hours as man and wife had confirmed that. I couldn't imagine any scenario without her by my side, refused to conceive a life without my exuberant blonde.

No man could come between us. Especially not a low life like Morrison.

"I'm scared." Tears brimmed in her eyes.

"Hey."

Tilting my head in her direction, I kissed her forehead tenderly. I wished I could touch her, hold her hand—do anything to assuage her obvious concern—but with my hands bound behind me, it was hopeless.

When I'd had Hilary at my mercy, I'd been able to do anything I wanted to her. I'd taken those times for granted—taken *her* for granted—but pressed against her in the back of the claustrophobic vehicle, I knew I'd never make the same mistake again. When I got us out of Morrison's grasp—and I *would* get us out of it—I would never make the mistake again.

"Are you going to let this slide?"

I tensed at the sound of Connor's voice again, my gaze returning to him reluctantly.

"Leave them alone."

Morrison was satisfyingly demoralized. The night clearly hadn't gone the way he'd expected either. It was the one slim silver lining of the whole sorry experience.

"What?" Connor snorted. "How can you let him coo over her like that?"

Morrison's gaze slid to Hilary and me. "He's her husband."

There was neither joy nor condemnation in his tone.

"Saul." Hilary leaned past me, catching Morrison's eyes. "Saul, don't do this. Just let us go."

Stretching back in his chair, he turned away from her. "It's too late for that."

"It's not too late!" She pulled in a shaky breath. "Everyone here has made mistakes, but why walk straight into another one?"

"You know me better than that." Disgust radiated from his voice, the stare he threw Hilary viscous. "You know everything I do is thought through and considered."

"This?' Hilary raised her bound hands into the air. She had the distinct advantage of having hers cuffed in front of her. *This is considered?* The man I knew would have understood he messed up, would have realized it was over. The man I knew would have walked away."

"That's bull," Connor grumbled. "The Syndicate doesn't walk away from anything."

"Except me." Her words lingered in the dark interior. "The Syndicate doesn't walk away from anything, *except me.*"

Her glare spoke of recriminations. "You walked away from me, Saul. You left me after I was abducted. How could you?" Hilary pulled in a breath, but this time I could tell it was fury pulsing through her veins, not fear. "How could you do that?"

"We had this conversation already." A glimmer of guilt glinted in Morrison's eyes.

"And you had no answer." She practically spat the words. "And now it's done."

Her gaze glided to mine. "I'm married. I'm no longer yours."

My cock swelled at her admission. Despite everything

that was going on, all the trauma and adrenaline of the last hour, there was still electricity when our gazes locked.

"Listen." Saul sighed. "I'm not saying I don't have any regrets, but I can't just let you go."

"Why?" She raised her voice, but her eyes never left mine. "It's the least you owe me."

"And what about him?"

I imagined Morrison's disdainful expression as he gestured to me.

"The man who kidnapped you. What does he deserve?"

"A chance of happiness." She pulled in a deep breath. "A chance to end this pointless gang violence and for both of you to leave each other alone."

"Enough of this!" Connor hissed. "I told you we should have covered their mouths with duct tape. I have plenty of it."

"That's your answer to everything, Reilly," Hilary sneered, cocking a brow at Morrison's man. "You take, you torment and you destroy."

Connor snorted. "You know nothing about me."

I glanced back in time to see his jaw tense.

"I know how you met Molly." Hilary's chest rose. "Know how you treated her."

"Shut up." Connor flashed her a glare. "Saul, make her shut up!"

"That's enough, all of you." Morrison lifted his hands in the air. "I can't think with all this noise."

I wanted to laugh at his performance. The man was weak, always had been. I knew precisely what I'd have done if the shoe had been on the other foot.

"We're going back to The Syndicate."

I rolled my eyes. "What a surprise."

"Saul." Hilary shook her head sadly. "It doesn't have to be this way."

I pulled in a breath as their gazes met.

"You're wrong, Hilary." Morrison's tone was miserable. "It has always been this way."

https://books2read.com/u/bOJ2xo

FOLLOW ME!

Stay in touch with Felicity's new releases by subscribing to her mailing list.
https://felicitybrandonwrites.com/newsletter/
You'll also receive FREE reads just for signing up!
Love Dark Romance?

Discover ALL The Dark Necessities **universe!**
https://books2read.com/u/mdGvJd

-

Devour Tempted for FREE:
https://books2read.com/u/b5kPPA

-

Join Felicity's Facebook group, **and Discord group, to engage with her and other awesome readers.**